Follow the Money

A Rick Bishop Novel, #4

Larry Darter

FEDORA PRESS

Contents

1. An Unexpected Visitor 1

2. Blast From the Past 4

3. Big Store 8

4. The Gorgeous Cousin 13

5. The Maui Charter 18

6. The Villa 23

7. Wake Up Call 28

8. Alex Baker in the Flesh 32

9. The Great Escape 37

10. Rescue Me 40

11. The Rendezvous 44

12. The Double-Cross 48

13. Back to Lahaina 53

14. Lodging Difficulties 57

15. Roomies 61

16. Two Can Play That Game 67

17. Facing the Music 71

18. Remember Pearl Harbor 75

19. Meanwhile 82

20. Abigail's Plot 87

21. The Tangled Web We Weave 90

22. Contact 97

23. Wasted Days and Wasted Nights 100

24. What to Do 105

25. Inspiration Strikes   108

26. Women Scorned   115

27. Frustration   119

28. Setting the Trap   123

29. Rock and Roll   128

30. Closing the Loop   133

31. Epilogue   136

About Author   140

Also By Larry Darter   141

CHAPTER ONE

An Unexpected Visitor

RETURNING FROM THE COFFEE shop on Bishop Street, Alex Baker took the elevator up to the sixteenth floor of the City Financial Tower building on Merchant Street. He stepped off the elevator and dug inside his pocket for his keys. Then he set off down the corridor to his office. As he approached, he saw a man leaning against the wall next to the office door, and Baker almost dropped his coffee cup. The man looked at him with the hint of a smile on his lips. Baker felt as though someone had gut-punched him, but he smiled and tried to hide his sudden attack of anxiety. The elevator had already gone back down, and he'd have to make it past the man to get to the fire stairs. There was no escape possible at the moment.

"Hello, Alex," the man said.

"Imagine seeing you standing here outside my office," Baker said. "Small world."

"Not really," the man said, pushing off the wall. "I've had good reason to see a lot of the world recently. Los Angeles, Mazatlan, Singapore, Bangkok, Sydney, and now Honolulu."

Baker took a sip of coffee, burning his upper lip.

"Travel is good times, isn't it?" Baker said, still smiling.

"It is now, Alex," the man said, stepping closer to Baker.

"Forgive me for keeping you standing out here in the corridor cooling your heels," Baker said. "I just ran down to the coffee shop. Let's go inside. I'm sure we have a lot to talk about."

"A great deal," the man said firmly.

"Yes," Baker said nervously.

"After you," the man said, gesturing toward the door.

Baker nodded, unlocked the glass door, and pushed inside with the visitor at his heels. They crossed the small reception area and passed through an open doorway into a lavishly furnished inner office with plush carpeting.

The visitor glanced around the room.

"It's quite an elaborate front you have here, Alex."

"Yes, well, you must maintain the illusion."

"Um-hum," the visitor agreed, walking over to and inspecting a closed steel door encased by a metal frame.

Baker hurried over as the visitor stepped toward the door and grabbed him by the upper arm.

"Uh, why don't you sit down?" Baker said, gesturing to the chairs in front of the large wooden desk. "And we'll have that talk."

But the visitor remained rooted to the floor, staring at the closed door.

"Would you care for a drink?" Baker said.

"No, thanks," the man said, looking over his shoulder at Baker. "What's in there?"

"Oh, it's only a storage closet."

"Um-hum," the man said, walking to the closet and trying the doorknob.

"Nothing in there, I guess?" the visitor said.

"Not at the moment. It's empty."

"If it's empty, why have you locked it?"

"Oh, it's only my habit, keeping things locked when not in use."

"Do you mind opening it?" the man said.

Baker looked at the visitor with a wry grin as the man slipped his right hand inside his jacket pocket.

"No, not at all," Baker said, removing his keys from his pocket again. Then he walked to the door and unlocked it.

"It is empty, I assure you," Baker said as he turned the knob and opened the door a crack.

The visitor shoved him aside roughly with his left hand, grabbed the edge of the door, and yanked it open. Then he stepped inside the closet and felt along the inside wall for a light switch. Baker swiftly slammed the door shut and locked it, trapping the visitor inside. Immediately, the man started pounding on the door, shouting at Baker to open the door.

"I'm terribly sorry," Baker shouted back. "But I just remembered I have an appointment to get to." Then he strode from the room, went out the exterior office door, and locked it behind him.

Baker exited the front door of the City Financial Tower building and stepped onto the sidewalk, only for another chilling sight to greet him. Three men got out of a white rental sedan parked at the curb across the street. Baker turned away and hurried down the sidewalk. When he heard one man shout his name, he sprinted the rest of the way to a red Aston Martin convertible parked at the curb, ecstatic that he had left the top down when he'd parked it earlier that morning. Baker put a hand on the passenger door window frame and vaulted into the front seat. He slid behind the wheel, stuck the key in the ignition, and started the car. Then he hit the accelerator and sped away with tires squealing. The three men had turned and ran back to their car. But by the time they got back inside the sedan, Baker was long gone.

Chapter Two

Blast From the Past

Bishop was bucks up.

He had just collected a very large recovery fee from a wealthy, shady businessman turned artist who could easily afford it for solving a large insurance fraud case. He was sitting at his shopworn office desk on a warm summer morning with the window open behind him, looking at his checkbook, admiring his bank balance, and thinking about whether he should buy a new car to replace his 1996 Toyota Corolla or take another vacation with Koko, his sweetheart. Then the phone rang. Bishop picked up the receiver.

"Honolulu Confidential and Discreet Investigations, this is Rick Bishop speaking."

"Rick Bishop, you dirty dog," a male caller said. "This is Alex. Alex Baker. How the hell are you, bud?"

Alex Baker? The name sounded familiar. Bishop's memory banks went into overdrive. Then he remembered. Alex Baker was a heavy weapons operator in Bishop's SEAL team platoon during his first deployment in the Pech District of Kunar Province, Afghanistan. Bishop had always liked Baker, a native Californian who always had a big smile on his face, no matter the circumstances.

"Alex!" Bishop exclaimed. "What's it been, brother? Ten years since I've seen you?"

Baker chuckled. "Yeah, dude, about that."

"You still living in California?"

"No, man, I'm living right here in the Paradise of the Pacific."

"Where?"

"Honolulu."

"Since when?"

"Oh, six months, maybe."

"Then why have I heard nothing from you until now?"

"Well, I've just been so damn busy, Rick. A pardner and I started a private equity firm here. I'm the managing partner, and it was tough going until we got established."

"You're a financial guy?"

"Yeah! Can you believe it? I went to college after I left the Navy and got a degree in finance. Then I got my Chartered Financial Analyst certification a few years ago."

"That's impressive," Bishop said. "So, how's business?"

"Oh, it's terrific now. Profits are literally going through the roof."

"Happy to hear it," Bishop said, wondering if Baker had called, hoping to lure him in as an investor client.

"Hey, Rick, I heard you left the cops and have your own private investigations shop," Baker said. "I was hoping to buy you lunch and to see if you might help me out with a minor problem."

"Sure, if I can," Bishop said, relieved to learn it wasn't a marketing call. "What's the trouble?"

"I can't get into it on the phone right now," Baker said. "I've got a client who should arrive any minute for a meeting. But if you're available for lunch, let's meet at the Prince Leleiohoku Club at noon, my treat. We can catch up over lunch, and I'll tell you all about the problem I need help with."

"Sounds great. I'll be there."

"Terrific, bud," Baker said. "See you there."

"Okay."

"Thanks, Rick," Baker said, and then he hung up.

Bishop replaced the handset on the phone cradle. That had been a surprise. Alex Baker had never struck him as a financial wizard. Yet his old friend from the teams must do all right by himself. Only Honolulu's wealthiest citizens could gain membership to the Prince Leleiohoku Club, or afford it, for that matter. Bishop had only been inside the club once before as the lunch guest of another member. And he looked forward to having lunch there again. Rick knew he'd also enjoy catching up with Alex. Life had certainly taken a turn for the better for Bishop over the past month. Maybe his luck had finally changed.

Bishop got off the bus two blocks from the Prince Leleiohoku Club on Kalakaua Avenue. On the off chance that Alex waited for him outside the club's entrance, Bishop didn't want his friend to see him disembarking from a city bus. Also, loathing the idea of his friend seeing him driving up in his old beater, Bishop had taken the bus instead of driving. Pride was a terrible thing. But since it appeared Alex had become a raging success, Bishop hadn't been able to help himself.

On foot, he arrived at the club at eleven-fifty, ten minutes ahead of the noon lunch date. Bishop heard someone call his name as he turned off the sidewalk toward the front door. He turned his head to see a smiling man climbing out of a red Aston Martin convertible parked in the club's driveway. Immediately, Bishop recognized his old friend Alex Baker. Baker strode over, grabbed Bishop's right hand, and pumped it enthusiastically. Then he gave Bishop a bro hug.

"So good to see you again, bud."

"You too, Alex," Bishop said, genuinely happy to see Alex again. "Ready to go inside?"

"Oh, I'm sorry, Rick," Baker said, frowning. "Something has come up, and I have to cancel. But we'll have lunch together soon. I just didn't want to be a no-show."

"Oh, okay," Rick said. "So, what about the problem you mentioned?"

"We'll talk about it later," Alex said, reaching into his pocket. He took out a key. "But if you don't mind, I have a small favor to ask."

"Sure, okay."

Alex offered Bishop the key. "There is a guy locked inside a closet back at my office. It's on the sixteenth floor of the City Financial Tower building. Do you know it?"

"Yes," Bishop said, hesitantly accepting the key. "On Merchant Street."

"Great," Alex said with a broad smile. "If you could go there and let him out, I'd appreciate it." Baker gave Bishop the suite number.

"But what's this about, Alex?" Bishop said. "Why is a man locked inside a closet at your office?"

"I'll explain everything later," Baker said. "Are you free this evening?"

"Yes, I guess so. I mean, I don't have any plans at the moment."

"Terrific. Then we'll get together, and I'll buy you dinner to make up for lunch. Then I'll explain everything. And, Rick, don't worry. I'm paying for your time starting now. So please keep track of your time and expenses and put them on the bill. We're friends, but I don't expect any special treatment. Whatever your usual rate is will be fine with me."

"Well, okay, but—"

Screeching tires arrested Bishop's attention, and he looked over his shoulder to see a white sedan careening around the corner onto Kalakaua Avenue. A city bus pulled away from the curb in front of the speeding car. The driver of the car slewed the sedan to the right to avoid colliding with the bus. The car bounced over the curb and slammed into a fire hydrant, knocking it over and sending a column of water shooting into the air.

"Right," Baker said. "I've got to run now, bud. But I'll get word to you about where to meet me this evening."

"Okay, but—"

Bishop didn't finish the thought, as Baker had already turned and sprinted back to the Aston Martin. He jumped inside, put the sports car in gear, and shot out of the driveway onto Kalakaua. Hearing shouts, a dumbfounded Bishop looked over his shoulder again and saw three men had emerged from the white sedan and were running toward him. Or they were running toward the Aston Martin, to be exact. When they saw the car speeding away, the men slid to a stop and stood on the sidewalk cursing after the recently departed Alex Baker. Then they turned and strolled back towards the wrecked sedan.

Shaking his head, Bishop crossed the street and walked to a bus stop, trying to recall which bus route City Financial Tower was on and what he was getting himself into by taking the job from Alex Baker.

CHAPTER THREE

Big Store

BISHOP EXITED THE BUS at the stop across from City Financial Tower. After crossing the street, he went inside the building, got in the elevator, and rode it up to the sixteenth floor. He found the suite Baker leased and saw a painted sign on the glass door: Pacific Paradise Partners. After unlocking the door with the key Baker had given him, Bishop entered the office suite. Immediately, he heard muffled shouts coming from an interior office. When he entered the private office, the shouts increased in volume.

"Baker, come back and open this door! Let me out of here!" Banging on the interior side of the metal door accompanied the desperate shouts.

The same key fitted the closet door lock.

"Hang on, I'll get you out," Bishop shouted back as he turned the key, grabbed the knob, and opened the door.

A red-faced man with sweat pouring from his brow, wearing a heather gray sports coat and charcoal pants, burst out of the closet.

"I could have suffocated in there," the man exclaimed. Then he looked at Bishop in confusion.

"Oh, thanks," he said finally. Then he turned and started toward the office door.

"Hey, wait a minute," Bishop said. "What's going on here?"

"Isn't it obvious?" the man said, turning back to glare at Bishop. "I was locked in that closet."

"Well, how did it happen?"

"Accident," the man said testily. "Now, if you'll excuse me, I have urgent business with Alex Baker. Where is he?"

"I don't know."

"You must know. It's obvious he gave you the key to this office. You must have seen him."

"He met me in town, gave me the key, and asked me to come here to let you out of the closet. Then he left. That's all I know, and I don't know where Alex went when he left me."

"All right, fine," the man said, and then he stormed out of the office.

Bishop shrugged when he heard the outer door open and shut. Then he looked around at the fancy office. Pacific Paradise Partners looked like a profitable affair. Bishop walked to the desk and saw a leather-bound appointment book on the desktop. He picked it up and flipped through it. Every page in the book was blank. He didn't find a single appointment entered. Also, some pages stuck together as if no one had ever opened the book before. Something seemed odd about the place, and Bishop's suspicions grew.

He walked behind the desk and opened the drawers one by one. He found every drawer empty, except for a bottom drawer that held a half-full bottle of scotch and two glasses. Next, walking to a row of expensive-looking wooden file cabinets along a wall next to the desk, Bishop opened and checked the drawers. There were labels on the front of each drawer, but none contained any files. Last, Bishop returned to the closet, found a light switch on an inside wall, and flipped it on. Like the desk and file cabinets, the closet was empty. Bishop realized then that the office was only an elaborate front. Obviously, the office was only a "Big Store," a confidence technique for selling the legitimacy of a scam where con artists furnished a leased space to look like a legitimate and substantial business. Pacific Paradise Partners was not a real company, which could mean only one thing. Alex Baker ran some scam and only used the fancy office to project an illusion of legitimacy.

Shaking his head, Bishop left the office, locking the door behind him, and then went back down to the lobby and across the street to the bus stop. Waiting for the bus, he wondered what Alex Baker had dragged him into and what Baker's con was. And who was he scamming?

Rick got off the bus a block down from the Likelike Club, a bar his best friend Joe Rose owned. Joe had named the club in honor of Hawaiian Princess Miriam Likelike, pronounced LEE-kay-LEE-kay, the sister of King Kalakaua and Queen Liliuokalani, Hawaii's last reigning monarchs. Koko Mahelona, Bishop's girlfriend, worked at the Likelike, where she was the bar manager and day shift bartender.

When Bishop walked in, he saw his friend Joe sitting at the bar in his usual corner, reading the paper. Joe turned slightly on his stool and peered at Bishop over the top of the newspaper.

"Hey, Richard," Rose said. "Koko is in the back checking in a delivery."

Bishop crossed the room and sat on a stool beside Rose.

"I'm not here to see Koko. I came to see you."

"About what?"

"Guess who I ran into today, Joe?"

"Richard, you know I hate guessing games. So either tell me who you saw or don't."

"My, aren't you the grumpy one today?"

"I'm not grumpy. I just don't have time for guessing games, pal."

"Okay, fine," Bishop said. "Do you remember Alex Baker from the platoon when we were in Kunar Province on our first deployment to the Stan?"

"Yeah, the heavy weapons operator, right?"

"That's right. Well, that's who I ran into today."

"I thought Alex was in California," Rose said. "Is he on vacation or what?"

"No, Alex says he moved here about six months ago to open a private equity firm."

"A private equity firm? The only thing I recall Alex knew about money was how to spend it in a hurry."

"Well, he claims he got a finance degree after he left the Navy, and that's he's now the managing partner at a firm called Pacific Paradise Partners."

"Huh? I have a lot of trouble imagining Alex Baker as some financial guru, but more power to him," Rose said.

"But here's the thing. I just came from his office. It looks legit on the surface, but I poked around the office a little and figured out that Alex's company is a fake. I found an appointment book on his desk containing no entries. The desk is empty. There aren't even any office supplies in it. And Alex has an entire row of expensive wooden filing cabinets that don't contain a single file. It's all an elaborate front."

"Why were you searching his office?"

"Alex gave me a key and asked me to go to his office to free a guy locked inside a closet at his office. After I let the guy out, things seemed suspicious, so I looked around."

"A guy locked in a closet? Who was he, and why did Alex lock him in the closet?"

"Dunno," Bishop said. "The guy stormed out after I freed him without telling me anything."

"And Alex explained none of it when he gave you the key?"

"No, we're supposed to meet for dinner this evening, and he promised to fill me in."

"Huh? It sounds weird to me. So you think Alex is running some con, and the business is only window dressing to make it look legit?"

"It certainly looks that way."

Koko walked in from the back. "Hey, babe," she said to Bishop.

"Hi, sweetheart," Rick said. "Working hard?"

"Just getting a delivery checked in," Koko said, grabbing a Longboard Island Lager from the refrigerator. She pulled the top from the bottle and set the beer on the bar in front of Rich.

"Thanks," Bishop said, smiling appreciatively. He drank some beer.

"What brings you here?" Koko said. "No work today?"

"I just stopped by to talk to Joe about one of our buds from the teams. I bumped into him today."

"Oh? Do I know him?"

"No, I haven't even seen him in about ten years. But his name is Alex Baker. He called me out of the blue this morning, and we were supposed to have lunch. But something came up, and he canceled. And I think he's in some kind of trouble."

"Like trouble he needs your help with?"

"I don't know yet. He hired me, but I don't even know what it's about yet."

Bishop took another pull on the bottle.

"I'd be careful if I were you, Richard," Rose said. "Alex was always a magnet for trouble, and he may be into something you shouldn't let him drag you into, pal."

"Is this Alex Baker a crook?" Koko said.

Bishop shrugged. "I don't know what he's into, but he's a friend and a brother. So I figure I at least owe it to Alex to hear what he has to say before I decide about helping him out."

"Where are you meeting him this evening?" Rose said. "Maybe I should tag along."

"I don't know that either," Bishop said. "Alex said he'd get in touch and let me know. That reminds me. I didn't have the chance to give him my cell phone number. So I better get back to the office. The office number is the only way he can reach me."

Bishop finished his beer and stood up.

"So, will you be at home when I get off work?" Koko said.

"Not sure, babe," Bishop said. "If Alex calls and I go to meet him this evening, I may be late."

"Okay," Koko said, not bothering to hide her irritation. Lately, Rick's work had been cutting into their time alone together.

Bishop leaned over the bar and gave Koko a quick kiss. Then he lifted a hand to Rose and left the club.

"I liked it better when Rick didn't have many cases," Koko said to Rose. "He's always getting home late or out of town these days, and I'm sick of it."

"You should be happy he's working for change," Rose said. "It seems Richard is finally serious about making something of himself."

"I suppose," Koko said. "At least he isn't broke all the time like he was before."

"There you go," Rose said. "That's something. It's not nothing."

CHAPTER FOUR

The Gorgeous Cousin

WHEN BISHOP GOT BACK to his Hotel Street office, he made coffee using the gently used single-cup brewer he had picked up for a song from the Goodwill store on South Beretania Street. Rick did much of his shopping at the store, since his earnings as a private investigator had been rather meager until just recently. He still bought his underwear at Walmart, since wearing someone's used drawers seemed more than a little disgusting, even to Bishop. But he bought used slacks, sports coats, shoes, and even office furnishings at Goodwill. That had saved him tons of money. And the stuff he bought still had a lot of good wear left in them.

Bishop drank coffee and perused new cars on the web while he awaited word from Alex Baker. Rick needed a new ride in the worst way. His ancient Corolla was on its last legs, and Bishop spent more on keeping the crankcase topped off with motor oil than he spent on gas. He had bought the Toyota used from a friend after wrecking his uninsured 4Runner that he was still making payments on to the bank. But thanks to his recent financial windfall, he finally had enough to pay off that loan and enough left over to put ten percent down on new wheels.

After three cups of coffee and almost two hours of trying to decide whether he wanted to buy a new Camaro or a Mustang, Rick had grown bored. The ancient clock on the wall, another Goodwill find, said it was going on four in the afternoon, but even so, Alex hadn't called. Of course, the clock was dependably five minutes slow, but Bishop had only paid four bucks for it, so five minutes slow from the timepiece wasn't bad.

Tired of coffee, Rick retrieved a bottle of Evan Williams Single Barrel from the bookshelf next to his desk and poured two fingers into a water tumbler. Then he propped his feet on his desk and sipped the bourbon. Bishop knew many whiskey drinkers shied away from Single Barrel because they associated the Evan Williams brand name with the lowest prices and quality. But Rick considered it the high end of that brand and found the bourbon delicate, gentle, and fruity. It was elegant sipping whiskey people shouldn't dismiss so quickly.

Bishop had almost finished his drink when his office door opened, and a busty woman breezed in—roughly 30, but ageless, with child-like eyes, dark brown, lush hair, and a thin, beautiful mouth slightly curved into a self-satisfied smile. She wore a navy dress with a hemline that ended well above her knees, offering a generous view of her gorgeous, shapely legs.

"Rick Bishop, I presume?" the woman said.

"That's me," Rick said, getting to his feet in such a hurry he almost knocked the whiskey bottle off the desk. "What can I do for you, Ms.—"

"Stone, Abigail Stone," the woman said with a bright smile.

She was fair-skinned and beautiful, although the word didn't even begin to do her justice.

"I don't have an appointment, but I hope you will make an exception and see me, anyway."

"Of course, Ms. Stone," Bishop said, gesturing toward a chair. "Please sit down."

"Thank you and please call me Abby. All my friends do."

Stone sat down and crossed her legs, which caused the short dress hem to rise even higher, exposing the darker-colored stocking top on her right leg and setting Bishop's heart aflutter. She didn't seem to notice.

"What can I do for you?" Bishop said, walking around the desk and leaning on the front edge of the desktop.

"Help my cousin. He's in terrible trouble."

"Of course. Who's your cousin?"

"Alex Baker. He speaks of you as an old and trusted friend. The only one he can turn to for help with his troubles."

"Alex's mistake, it seems, wasn't telling anyone he had a cousin like you, Ms. Stone. Otherwise, I'm sure he'd have friends lining up to help. I don't recall him mentioning having an attractive cousin named Abigail."

Stone beamed. "Well, thank you, Rick. That's kind of you. I may call you Rick, can't I? Alex has spoken of you so often that I feel as though I already know you. And please, you must call me Abby. I insist."

"All right, Abby."

Alex and I are very close, but sometimes I don't see him for a year or more. He moves around quite a bit."

"Yes, I saw him moving pretty fast this afternoon," Bishop said. "With three men moving right along behind him."

"Oh, no!" Stone exclaimed.

"Abby, you said Alex was in trouble. Were you unaware that some men are chasing him?"

Stone frowned and made a helpless gesture. "Why? Why can't they leave him alone?"

"Who are they?"

"I don't know," Stone said sadly. "All I know is they have mercilessly hounded poor Alex. They've followed him halfway around the world."

"If you don't know the men's identities, I suppose you don't know why they're hounding him."

"No, sorry."

"And you wouldn't know anything about Pacific Paradise Partners or what the company's business might be?"

"I'm afraid not," Stone said. "But you will help us, won't you, Rick? Cousin Alex is counting on you."

"Where did Alex call you from, Abby?"

"Maui. From a hotel he's staying at, he said."

"What else did he say?"

"Alex said those men had truly run him to ground this time. And if you couldn't help him, it might be the end of everything for him. Alex is desperate for your help, and he instructed me to tell you that money is no object."

Bishop smiled. "Well, it isn't for me either, Abby. Alex is a friend. We served together. I want to help him if I can. It's just that I'm trying to figure out what's going on, you know? For instance, why does Alex need my help? Why doesn't he just go to the police?"

Stone stood up and stepped closer to Bishop. She placed a hand on his arm.

"Won't you please come with me now?" she pleaded earnestly. "I'm sure Alex will explain everything to your satisfaction. But we're wasting precious time."

"All right, Ms. Stone," Bishop said in a husky voice.

"Abby," Stone said with a coquettish smile, her hand lightly stroking Bishop's arm.

Bishop grinned and nodded. "Abby," he said.

"Cousin Alex was right," Stone said.

"About what?"

"You," Stone said with another flirtatious smile, her lips slightly brushing Bishop's lips before she turned her head and kissed him lightly on the cheek.

"So, are we headed to the airport?" Bishop stammered.

"Oh, God, no," Stone said. "We haven't time for a commercial flight. However, I'm prepared to pay for a helicopter charter if you can recommend a good service to fly us to Maui."

"Well," Bishop said hesitantly. "There are several good helicopter charter services to choose from near the Ala Wai Canal."

Among the helicopter services was Makai Island Hopper, owned by Bishop's former friend, a woman named Gabby Inouye. When Bishop became enamored with Gabby, a truly beautiful woman, he had engaged in a little harmless flirtation. But Gabby had taken it for more than Bishop had intended and became obsessed with the desire to sleep with him. But Bishop, who couldn't imagine cheating on Koko, had tried to steer things back to the friend zone with Gabby. Then she became, in her mind, a woman scorned and had made things hard for Bishop ever since. Rick had even recently spent two weeks in Maui hiding from Gabby while pretending to be on the mainland on a case. He'd even lied to Koko about his whereabouts because Gabby and Koko were close friends. Bishop intended to avoid Gabby and Makai Island Hopper like the bubonic plague.

"Marvelous," Stone said, interrupting Bishop's thoughts. "Shall we go then?"

"Sure," Bishop said.

"I came by taxi," Stone said. "We'll have to take your car."

"Swell," Bishop said, groaning inwardly. "It's in my reserved parking space behind the building."

Stone and Bishop went downstairs and exited onto the sidewalk. Bishop's landlady, Mrs. Wong, the owner of the Chinese herbal shop below Rick's office, was sweeping the sidewalk in front of her store with a fan broom. She glanced up at them and then glared at Bishop.

"Mr. Rick, remember rent is due in two days. You pay on time."

"Yes, Mrs. Wong, I haven't forgotten," Bishop said in embarrassment.

"And, Mr. Rick, your old car leak oil all over the alley behind the building. You clean up oil, Mr. Rick, before the city fine me. You hear?"

"Yes, Mrs. Wong," Rick said over his shoulder as he took Stone by the arm and guided her gently away in the opposite direction.

"Who was that?" Stone said.

"Mrs. Wong, my landlady," Rick said. "Poor thing. Like our pathetic old president, she is in the final stages of advanced dementia and doesn't even know what's she saying."

The pair walked around the building to the alley in the back of Bishop's building. He escorted Stone to the Toyota and opened the passenger door. Stone looked inside, glanced at Bishop dubiously, and wrinkled her nose.

"This is your car?"

Rick grinned encouragingly. "It's a loaner. My car is in for an oil change, and I use a small independent garage to support the little guy. So, my mechanic doesn't have much of a selection where loaners are concerned."

"I see," Stone said, getting gingerly into the front seat.

Rick closed the door and started around to the other side when he noticed someone had piled plastic bags of garbage on the car's hood. Glancing at the dumpster, he saw it overflowed with refuse, which explained why they had used Rick's car for auxiliary garbage disposal. Bishop cast the smelly bags on the ground and got behind the wheel.

With a silent prayer, Rick turned the ignition key, and the Corolla's engine shuddered to life. After an ear-splitting backfire, dense black smoke from the exhaust blanketed the alley. Stone, who had rolled down the passenger door window against the heat, began coughing as though subjected to tear gas. Grimly, Bishop reversed out of the parking space and then drove down the alley, leaving the noxious smoke and odors of burning motor oil in their wake. Rick turned onto Hotel Street and made for the Ala Wai Canal at best speed as the Corolla's engine howled in protest.

CHAPTER FIVE

The Maui Charter

THERE WERE THREE CHARTER helicopter services lining the street that ran parallel with the canal. Makai Island Hopper was at the end of the street. Bishop drove into the parking lot belonging to the first service. When he switched off the ignition, the engine rattled, banged, and issued another loud backfire before a prolonged period of dieseling began.

Bishop and Stone got out of the car and walked into the office. There they found a man wearing a flight suit sitting behind a desk. He introduced himself as Steve Jackson and asked if he could help them.

"We need a charter to Maui," Bishop said.

"When?" Jackson said.

"Right away," Stone said. "It's something of an emergency."

"Oh, sorry," Steve said. "I'd like to help you folks, but a party of four has scheduled a sunset tour for this evening. Unfortunately, I couldn't make it to Maui and back in time."

"Okay, thanks anyway," Bishop said. "Guess we'll check next door."

"Don't waste your time," Jackson said. "Jack's bird is down for maintenance. But you might check with Gabby Inouye at the end of the street. I ran into her at the post office this afternoon, and she mentioned getting a tour cancellation. So she can probably take you to Maui. And Gabby has night flight certification, so it will be no problem for her to make the return trip after dark."

"Wonderful," Stone said. "Thanks so much, Steve."

Then Stone and Bishop left the office.

"Maybe we should try one of the services out at the airport," Bishop said.

"Whatever for, Rick? Steve said the pilot down the road could take us. Don't tell me you have an issue with female helicopter pilots."

"No, not that," Bishop said. "You see, Gabby Inouye and I share a history. An unhappy history."

"Is she an ex-girlfriend?"

"Not exactly, but she wanted to date me. I already had a girlfriend, and I'm not the cheating kind. But Gabby wouldn't take no for an answer when I refused to sleep with her. When I stood my ground, she adopted a scorned woman attitude. And I guess you know how that turns out for the guy the woman believes scorned her."

"Did you? Scorn her, I mean?"

"No, not at all. It was all a horrible misunderstanding that turned into almost a fatal attraction thing."

"Oh my," Stone said. "But under the circumstances, I think you'll have to man up and face her, Rick. We really must get to Maui as soon as possible."

Bishop sighed. "Well, we can ask if you insist, but I doubt Gabby Inouye would fly me to a hospital if I were bleeding to death."

"Oh, don't be so dramatic, Rick," Stone chuckled. "Besides, I'll be hiring her, not you."

When they got back to the Toyota, Rick discovered it had overheated and wouldn't start, so they walked down to Makai Island Hopper. Rick opened the door and allowed Stone to enter first in case Gabby armed herself and started shooting. At least having Stone as a human shield would give him a fighting chance to escape alive.

Gabby sat at her desk, doing paperwork. When she looked up and saw Bishop, she sprang to her feet, glowering at him.

"Richard Bishop, you lying, philandering bastard, get out of here this instant. We have nothing to say to each other."

Bishop could think of no adequate riposte in the face of Gabby's sudden gush of fury and vitriol. Stone stepped forward into the breach.

"Excuse me, Ms. Inouye," she said. "I understand there is some unpleasant history between you and Mr. Bishop. But I desperately need to get to Maui this afternoon and hope you'll consider letting me hire you."

Gabby looked at Stone.

"I'm Abigail Stone, by the way. I'm pleased to meet you."

"I'm available and happy to take you anywhere you care to go, Ms. Stone," Gabby said. "But not him. He isn't setting foot in my bird."

Stone looked at Gabby with equal parts of compassion and understanding. "Ms. Inouye. Gabby. As a woman, I know what unfeeling bastards that men can be. I'm sure you have every right to feel as you do about Mr. Bishop. But unfortunately, I have a cousin in Maui who is in dire straits, and he insists Mr. Bishop is the only one who can help him. So, Mr. Bishop must accompany me. If you would consider flying us to Maui, I'm happy to pay any price you require."

Gabby looked undecided. And so vulnerable, Rick thought. She had never looked more beautiful. Finally, she spoke to Stone.

"What do you want? A flight over and back?"

"Yes, but we will probably have to overnight," Stone said. "Besides the charter fee, I'll also pay for your lodging and meals if we have to stay over."

Gabby considered her lost revenues from the canceled afternoon's charter and that she had nothing definitely scheduled for the rest of the week.

"Okay," she said with a sigh. "On one condition. Bishop doesn't say a single word when he is in my presence."

"Deal," Stone said before turning to Bishop.

"Not one word, understand?"

Bishop nodded meekly.

"Okay," Gabby said. "I'll take you."

Stone and Gabby worked out the price, and then Stone paid her for the charter portion in cash.

"I'll go do my preflight. Meet me at the bird out back on the helipad in ten minutes."

"Thank you," Stone said. Then Gabby left the office through the back door.

"I'm sorry for throwing you under the bus like that," Stone said to Bishop. "She's quite the drama queen, but I'm desperate to get to Maui as soon as possible."

"Sure, I understood what you were doing," Bishop lied. "No worries."

"Are you still with the woman that came between you and Gabby?"

"Oh, no," Bishop said sadly. "She died in a tragic surfing accident."

"Oh my, how terrible that must have been for you."

"Yes, it's been a daily struggle to come to terms with the loss."

Stone threw her arms around Bishop, hugged him, and gave him another gentle kiss on the cheek.

Bishop chastised himself silently for the lie. Why did he allow attractive women like Abby to get to him? It seemed clear she wanted him, and he couldn't help wanting her. So the lie just slipped out before he had time to think about it. He dreaded the trip to Maui now. He felt too weak to remain strong for Koko's sake in the face of the temptation Abby Stone posed. After all, he was only human.

Abby and Bishop joined Gabby at her McDonnell Douglas 500E helicopter ten minutes later. Looking at Bishop with a hostile stare, Gabby jerked a thumb at the rear passenger compartment. Then she helped Stone situate herself in the front passenger seat. It was the seat Bishop had always occupied in the past. With a sigh, Bishop climbed in the back. Once they were all belted inside the bird, Gabby gave Stone a headset so they could communicate in flight but didn't offer one to Bishop. So it didn't matter if he said a word or not, since no one would hear him over the engine noise.

Gabby made her last-minute checks. Then she increased the throttle. The helicopter got light on its skids, lifted off, and then Gabby flew out over the Pacific towards Maui.

During the flight, Bishop realized Gabby's brutal treatment of him had hurt far more than he had expected. That made him realize he still had powerful feelings for her. Somehow, he had to get back into her good graces and win her back. He intended to work on that after seeing how things turned out with Abby Stone in Maui.

An hour after leaving Honolulu, Gabby landed the bird at the Kapalua airport on the west side of the Island of Maui. While she tended to the helicopter, Stone and Bishop went to the rental car counter. Stone rented two cars, one for her and Bishop and the other for Gabby. Then they returned to the terminal to meet Gabby. Stone handed Gabby the paperwork and the key to the second rental.

"I got you a rental to come and go as you wish," Stone said. "You know where we're staying, and I'll have arranged a room for you by the time you arrive."

"Thanks," Gabby said, eyeing Bishop. "Just make sure it's a room on a different floor from Bishop's room, in another wing, if possible."

Stone smiled. "I'll see what I can do."

After Stone and Gabby said goodbye, she and Bishop went to the lot and picked up their rental. Since he knew his way around Maui, Stone told him where they were going and that he should drive and then gave him the car key.

"If you did half the things that woman claims, you are a bastard, Rick," Stone chuckled.

Uh-oh, Rick thought. Gabby and Abby must have done a lot of talking on the flight over from Oahu. He only hoped that Gabby hadn't mentioned that Koko Mahelona hadn't died in any tragic surfing accident and was alive and well in Honolulu.

"Well, you only heard her side of the story," Bishop protested. "I'm sure she told it in the way that cast her in the best light. It was really only a huge misunderstanding. Nothing more."

"Huh? She told me you did your best to seduce her, and then when she gave in and was ready to do the deed, you refused. And then you dropped her like a bad habit."

"Well, see, it wasn't like that at all," Bishop said. "Gabby and I were good friends. Sure, I engaged in a little harmless flirting, as friends of the opposite sex often do, but Gabby made more of it than it was. Then she grew increasingly obsessive. She demanded I sleep with her and break up with my girlfriend to be with her."

"The girlfriend you lost to the tragic surfing accident?"

"Yes, but that tragedy happened after the events that Gabby related to you."

"Well, one thing is for sure. The only thing Gabby feels for you now is loathing."

"Yes, I got that. Now, can we talk about something more pleasant?"

"Yes, Rick. I imagine it can't be pleasant reliving your terrible experiences with Gabby. So, have you stayed at the Lahaina Beachfront Villas before?"

"Yes, I recently spent a two-week vacation there."

"Oh, how nice. Alex has rented a villa there. He said it's very roomy, so I'll probably stay there and rent rooms for you and Gabby."

"That works for me. You really think it will be necessary to overnight here?"

"Well, it makes sense to plan for it, although we won't know for sure until we see cousin Alex and learn more about his current circumstances."

"I guess you're right," Bishop said, knowing he needed to call Koko as soon as possible to let her know he wouldn't be back home until the following day.

CHAPTER SIX

The Villa

BISHOP TURNED OFF THE highway onto the access road leading to the Lahaina Beachfront Villas Resort. When he arrived at the parking lot in front of the main hotel building, he parked the rental and switched off the engine.

"You're sure Alex is staying at this resort?" Bishop said.

"Yes," Stone said.

"What now?"

"Cousin Alex said to go into the main lobby and wait for someone to contact us. I'll book rooms for you and Gabby, and then we'll make ourselves comfortable in the lobby to wait."

"Wait, for whom?"

"He said he'd have a man meet us there who would escort us to his villa."

"All right, let's do it," Bishop said.

They got out of the rental and went into the resort hotel's lobby. Bishop staked out two comfortable chairs near the center of the lobby while Abigail Stone went to the front desk to book the rooms. She returned a few minutes later and handed Bishop a key card tucked inside a cardboard folder with the room number printed on it. Bishop slipped it into his jacket pocket.

"Want me to find us some coffee while we wait?" Bishop said.

"I think it's better to wait here together for a while and see what develops. The man may be along at any time. He will look for a man and a woman together. I don't want to risk missing him."

"Okay," Bishop said, but still wishing he had some coffee.

They hadn't waited long before a smiling man wearing a colorful Aloha shirt over dark slacks approached them. Bishop thought the man looked like a hotel staff member.

"Ms. Abigail Stone?" the man said to Abby.

"Yes," Stone said.

The man nodded. "Please come with me?"

Stone made a move to get up, but Bishop reached out, grabbed her arm, and kept her sitting.

"Where?" Bishop said to the man.

"Please, sir, Mr. Baker gave me specific instructions."

"Is your name Kai?" Stone said.

The man nodded. "Yes, Kai Halia."

Stone turned to Bishop and smiled. "I'm sure it's all right." Then she got to her feet, and Bishop followed her lead.

Halia took Stone by the elbow in a friendly manner to escort her. "I'm so glad you've arrived," he said. "Your cousin is anxious. He feared you may have had an accident. He told me he was worried something had happened."

"Well, as you see, we're fine," Stone said.

"He will be so relieved," Halia said, escorting them through the lobby and then outside through a rear exit.

They passed a pool and patio area and then continued over the lush, manicured grounds toward a group of detached villas. Halia took them directly to the door of one villa and then opened the door without knocking and gestured them inside. Stone entered with Bishop following her, and Halia came inside behind him.

"Your cousin will be so happy that everything is all right," Halia said, and then he produced a snub nosed revolver from his waistband and touched the muzzle to the back of Bishop's neck.

"Please, do not move, sir," he said. "I'd not like to shoot you."

Stone turned and looked at Halia, open-mouthed.

"Abby, I thought you said once we got here, Alex would explain everything," Bishop said to Stone. "And I don't recall you mentioning anything about someone sticking a gun in my neck."

Two men walked into the room from a hallway.

"We will explain everything," one man said. "Don't worry about it."

Immediately, Bishop recognized the two men. They had gotten out of the wrecked white sedan with a third man when Bishop had met Alex Baker in front of the Prince Leleiohoku Club. Since he didn't like the odds, Bishop thought two against one sounded better than three against one, so he wheeled suddenly, slapped Halia's gun hand to the side, and slugged him in the face. The move surprised Halia, and he lost his grip on the gun and dropped it.

Bishop had already turned around to meet the new threat, and the two others were almost on him. Both seemed like solidly built guys with the looks of ex-military types.

Bishop took the first one out with a left hook. After he went down, Bishop slipped a straight right from the second guy and then countered with a left punch to the gut and a right uppercut. The uppercut snapped the man's head back on his neck, but he didn't go down. Instead, he grabbed the lapels of

Bishop's jacket and jerked him in close in a clinch to give himself time to shake off the effects of the solid punch.

Stone screamed, and Bishop glanced over his shoulder and saw Halia with his arm around her throat, dragging her backward out the door. Bishop knew he had to win the fight quickly if he was to rescue Stone. So, he stomped his right heel down on the guy's left instep, which caused the man to loosen his grip on Bishop's jacket. Then Bishop shoved the man away with his left hand and delivered a palm strike with his right hand beneath the man's left jaw. That staggered him, and Bishop started to throw a right hook to finish him. But the first guy was off the floor and back in the fight.

He got an arm bar around Bishop's neck from behind, and the second man hit Bishop in the face with a left, right combination. Bishop twisted and broke out of the arm bar and punched the guy behind him with a right jab. The man went down again, and Bishop turned to go back to work on the second guy. He hit him with a straight left and drew back his arm for a right cross. But the first guy was off the deck again. Having landed on the floor beside the gun that Halia had dropped, the man came up with it in his right hand. He struck Bishop on the head behind the right ear with the gun butt. Bishop slumped to the floor, unconscious.

Bishop woke up lying flat on his back on the floor of the villa with a painful headache. He reached back with his left hand and touched his head. He felt a large bump and his hand came away with blood on it. While he didn't know how long he had been out, he could tell from the dim lighting it was almost dark outside. Abigail Stone was long gone, and so was the reception committee.

With a groan, Bishop pushed himself up to a knee and then waited several moments for sudden dizziness to pass. Then he got shakily to his feet. Finally, he staggered over to a wet bar against a wall.

Inside the freezer of a small refrigerator, he found a container of ice cubes. He wrapped ice inside a bar towel and applied it to his aching head. Bishop started feeling better almost immediately. Then he heard someone opening the front door and ducked down behind the bar. He heard footsteps and the door shutting. Peeking around the corner of the bar, he recognized the man who had walked in. It was the guy he had freed from the closet in Alex's office. Slowly, Bishop stood up, still holding the ice-filled bar towel to his head.

"You look terrible," the man said.

"Thanks," Bishop said. "What are you doing here?"

"Following you."

"From Honolulu?"

"Yes."

"I thought you had urgent business with Alex Baker. Why are you following me?"

"I do and was hoping you and the woman would lead me to him."

"Look, just who are you, anyway?"

The man reached inside his jacket and produced a leather case. He flipped it open and held it out.

"Special Agent Craig Lynch, Naval Criminal Investigation Service."

"What does NCIS want with Alex Baker?"

"We want to apprehend the man who stole $10 million from the government, and naturally, we want to recover the money or what Baker has left of it."

"Stolen from where exactly?"

"Kabul."

"Afghanistan? When?"

"About five years ago."

"Alex left the Navy and the Stan years before then."

"That's true," Lynch said. "But he returned to Afghanistan in 2017 as a DOD contractor. And that's when he and three accomplices, also DOD contractors, hit a government finance storage facility in Kabul and took the money which belonged to the U.S. Department of State."

"Why is NCIS involved? It seems like the FBI should investigate something like that."

"It was State Department money, but they had stored it at a Navy facility we operated and guarded. The thieves also took out two Navy personnel guarding the site. So we have jurisdiction, not the FBI."

"How could four DOD contractors get $10 million out of Afghanistan?"

"It wasn't difficult back then. They only needed a contact inside the military supply chain in Afghanistan and one back here in the states. So Baker and his accomplices paid off someone to ship the money back to Long Beach, hidden inside a military shipping container. Then they paid off someone in Long Beach to access the container inside a secure military dockside facility and retrieved the money from the shipping container."

"Huh? You make it sound easy."

"Unfortunately, it was. But we arrested their Afghanistan contact, a Navy logistics specialist, on an unrelated charge, and he gave up Baker and the others to get a reduced sentence on the charge. And that's how we found out they stole the money, which the State Department had already reported missing."

"Why are you only after Baker? What about the others?"

"Oh, we plan to arrest them, too. But we're focused on Baker because he is the one who retrieved the money in Long Beach. And instead of sharing it with the others, Baker absconded with all the money. So, getting him is our best chance at recovering the $10 million, give or take a few hundred thousand, since we know he has already spent some of it."

"One more question. Why am I here?" Bishop said.

"What was Abigail Stone's reason for inviting you to come here to Maui with her?"

"I was supposed to rescue her cousin Alex from some very mysterious enemies," Bishop said. "Question two. Who is Abigail Stone?"

"A long-time, sometimes constant companion of Alex Baker. I've been watching her for over six months, hoping she would lead me to Baker. That's how I found him in Honolulu. And, for your information, he's no more her cousin than you are."

"Yeah," Bishop said. "I had almost figured that one out on my own."

"You should return to Honolulu," Lynch said. "No one would blame you."

"No, I think I'll stay here and try to find Abigail. She's still in trouble."

"She's not any trouble," Lynch said.

"Of course she is. I saw three men abduct her from this villa earlier."

"Oh, sure, Baker's former accomplices—Mark Preston and his associates. But once they learn Stone doesn't know where Baker is, they will let her go. They are thieves, not killers. And once they learn Baker is trying to contact you to help him, they will realize they abducted the wrong person. You would have been a far more valuable prize to Mr. Preston and his cohorts than Abigail Stone. They will understand that when they realize if they had abducted you they wouldn't have to look for Baker because he would have come looking for you. That's why my advice is to go back to Honolulu while you have the chance."

Bishop nodded, and Lynch turned and left the villa through the front door.

Bishop found a bottle of scotch on a shelf of the wet bar and poured himself a glass. He savored it while he contemplated his options. He was unconvinced that Abigail Stone was in no danger and couldn't bring himself to abandon her until he knew for sure she was okay. But before doing anything, he figured he'd sleep on it since he was overnighting in Maui, anyway.

Bishop wandered around the villa until he found the master bedroom. No one was using the villa, and the bed looked comfortable, so he saw no reason to walk all the way back to the hotel to sleep in the room Abby had rented for him. So after finishing the scotch, Bishop undressed, turned back the covers, and got into bed. Within minutes, he fell asleep.

CHAPTER SEVEN

Wake Up Call

IT WAS A GRAND Thursday morning in Maui when Bishop woke up. It was grand because he awakened to someone smothering his face with gentle kisses. There was just something about being kissed awake that Bishop had always liked. He opened his eyes to see it was Abby Stone doing the kissing. Since she was smiling down at him and looked no worse for the wear, Bishop closed his eyes and enjoyed her affectionate ministrations, wondering how far she intended to take things.

"Good morning," Abby said, between kisses.

"Good morning," Bishop said, his eyes still closed. "How did you get away?"

"I didn't."

Bishop snapped his eyes open as a man grabbed Abby's shoulders and pulled her roughly away. Then he sat up in bed and looked at the three men standing at the foot of the bed. Two had Abby standing between them, each hanging onto one of her arms. The third guy stood smirking with his arms crossed.

"Who are you?" Bishop said to the smirking guy. "How did you get in here?"

"Bishop, why all the hostility?" the man said. "That's gratitude for you. I could have had one of my boys slap you awake."

"I'm so sorry, Rick," Abby said. "For getting you involved in this."

"Take Ms. Stone out to the car," the smirking guy said to the other two.

"Hey, just hold it," Bishop said. "If you came here expecting me to help you find Alex Baker, let her go, or you're just wasting your time."

"Bishop, you're in no position to make demands."

"Either she walks out of here alone, or you'll get no cooperation from me, pal."

The man studied Bishop for a moment and then cracked a smile. "Well, I've always been a trusting soul, so all right." He turned to the men holding Abby. "Let her go."

The men released their grips on her arms. Abby looked disbelieving and didn't move for a moment. Then, deciding it wasn't a trick, she hurried to the bedroom door. Before exiting, she looked back over her shoulder and smiled at Bishop.

"Thank you, Rick," she said.

Bishop held up his hand and wiggled his fingers in a wave goodbye. Abby hurried out of the room and then was gone.

"Now, let's start at the beginning," Bishop said to the man, who was back to smirking. "Who are you?"

"My name is Preston. Mark Preston. My associates here, who you've met, have names, but that's of no interest to you. Your deal is with me."

"Deal? What sort of deal is that?"

"There's two thousand in it for you," Preston said. "You get one thousand up front just for agreeing to cooperate and doing what I ask. And earning the other thousand will be just as easy."

"Well, everyone has different definitions of the word easy."

Preston smiled again. "All I want you to do is to deliver a message to your friend for me. Alex Baker."

"Well, I can handle the first part of that. I take pride in being an agreeable, cooperative sort. But let's hear the message."

"I want you to tell Alex we have no hard feelings towards him and that we grabbed Abby last night, and we can do it again whenever we want unless he intends to give us our shares of the money, per our original agreement."

"Are you sure he won't make a counteroffer?" Bishop said.

"Counteroffer?"

"Yes, like you can have Abby, and he'll keep the money."

Preston chuckled. "Oh, no. Alex knows better than to play a game like that with me. He wouldn't want to accept responsibility for something bad happening to Abby."

"Huh? So, you're saying if Alex doesn't give you what you want, you'll hurt Abby?"

"Well, you know how it is, Bishop. Unfortunately, people have tragic accidents every day. But the important question is, are you going to deliver the message to Alex?"

"You know, here's the problem. I don't have a clue where to look for Alex to give him your message."

"Oh, that's no problem," Preston said. "I'll take you to him. Now, will you deliver the message?"

"If you know where Alexis is, why don't you just tell him yourself? Why do you need me?"

"I know where Alex is, but he won't see me. And because of a minor complication, I can't force him to see me. But he will see you."

"And if I refuse?"

"You seem like a smart guy, Bishop. I'm sure you can figure that one out. Wouldn't you rather earn an easy two thousand instead?"

"Okay, why not?" Bishop said. "I'm in."

"I thought you would say that," Preston said with a smile.

He reached inside his jacket and took out a wallet. Opening it, he pulled out ten one hundred-dollar bills and dropped them on the comforter that Bishop lay beneath on the bed. Then he turned to his associates.

"Okay, you guys can go." Both men turned and left the bedroom. Then Preston looked back at Bishop.

"Well, you better get dressed. We have a little drive ahead of us this morning."

Fifteen minutes later, Preston and Bishop were driving south along the coast on HI-30. About a half-hour later, they continued on the same highway when it curved to head due east.

"Where are we going?" Bishop said.

"The Iao Valley near the West Maui Forest Preserve," Preston said.

"What's there?"

"An abandoned sugar plantation from the old days," Preston said. "On lands managed by the Hawaii Department of Land and Natural Resources. Once the state took over the property, they allowed it to return to its natural state, so now it's a rain forest area that some people are using to cultivate cannabis."

"An illegal marijuana grow?"

"Precisely."

"What's Alex doing there?"

"Staying with some friends, the people cultivating the weed. They are some old friends of his from California who came here from the mainland because it's easy to get away with large-scale pot production in rural Hawaii."

"And they are the minor complication that prevents you from seeing Alex yourself."

"Yes, there are about a dozen of them, and as all the cannabis growers around here are, they are heavily armed."

"And you don't want to get shot."

"Right, but I also don't want a gunfight that would attract law enforcement out here."

From his time as a cop, Bishop knew people grew more illegal cannabis in Hawaii than in any other state. They had cultivated cannabis outdoors in Hawaii for decades because the tropical climate was conducive to year-round outdoor cultivation. Mostly, people cultivated cannabis extensively on vast tracts of unincorporated public lands managed by the Department of Land and Natural Resources.

DLNR wasn't a law enforcement agency and wouldn't risk violent confrontations with the armed growers. Law enforcement once did a good job of controlling illegal cannabis cultivation through aerial surveillance and eradication efforts. But now, local county councils restrained those efforts, citing complaints from many residents who reportedly opposed the program because low-flying helicopter surveillance missions violated their privacy and disrupted their rural lives. And law enforcement didn't have the manpower to mount meaningful eradication efforts without the aerial surveillance piece. So, illegal cultivation boomed with little interference.

Finally, Preston pulled off the highway onto a dirt road and followed it for about three miles before stopping the car where the dirt track entered a forested area.

"This is the place," Preston said, cutting the engine and getting out of the car. Bishop got out, too.

"The old plantation house is right down the road, about two clicks ahead," Preston said. "But this is far as I go. So you'll have to walk it. And that's where you will find Alex."

"I know dope growers aren't welcoming to people nosing around their grow sites," Bishop said. "What makes you think they won't shoot me?"

"They won't shoot you on sight," Preston said encouragingly. "They will give you a chance to explain what you're doing here. All you have to do is convince them you're a friend of Alex and that he wants to see you."

"You make it sound easy, but I don't share your optimism," Bishop said.

"Well, look at this way, Bishop. You walk to the house to deliver the message, and there's a good chance you won't get shot." Preston pulled back his jacket to reveal a semi-automatic in his waistband. "But if you renege on our deal, I'll gut shoot you and leave you here to bleed out. And that's a sure thing, champ."

"I see your point," Bishop said, glancing up the road. "Okay, I'm going."

"And I'll be right here waiting for you with the other thousand when you get back after delivering the message."

"How comforting," Bishop said, and then he turned and started walking.

CHAPTER EIGHT

Alex Baker in the Flesh

BISHOP STUCK TO THE middle of the road without trying to conceal himself. The last thing he wanted was for a bunch of armed pot growers to think he was sneaking around their grow site. At least it was a pleasant morning for a walk. The sky was blue, and the sun was shining through the trees. The temperature was in the low seventies. And he had a thousand dollars in his pocket he hadn't had yesterday.

About twenty minutes after leaving Preston, Bishop saw a two-story wood-frame house in a clearing ahead. It surprised him he'd made it to the house without running into any gun-toting pot farmers, but he'd had that uncomfortable feeling that someone had been watching him for a while—the feeling where the tiny hairs at the back of his neck seemed to stand on end. Then, just before he got to the clearing, he felt something hard jab him in the back.

"Hold it right there," a male voice said.

"What are you doing here?" another voice said.

Bishop instinctively put his hands up as soon as he felt the jab, since he was sure he knew what someone had pressed against his back.

"I'm Alex Baker's friend Rick," Bishop said. "He's in some trouble and asked me to come here to help."

"How do you know Alex?" one man said.

"We served in the Navy together."

"Are you law enforcement?"

"No, I'm a private investigator, and Alex hired me to help him."

Bishop felt hands patting him down for a weapon. Then someone told him to turn around. So he turned to face the two men. Both looked like California beach bums—long hair, sloppy clothes, and sunglasses. One, a tall skinny guy, held a high-powered hunting rifle. The other, a guy of average build, held a pump shotgun.

"How do we know you're who you claim?" one said.

"I've got identification in my wallet. It's in my hip pocket."

"Okay, let's see it."

Bishop took out his wallet and showed them his Hawaii state private investigator's license.

"You think this is the dude Alex mentioned?" one guy asked the other.

"Looks like it, bro."

"Okay, dude," the tall one said. "Turn and walk to the house up there. We'll see what Alex has to say."

Bishop complied, and a couple of minutes later, he stepped out of the trees into the clearing. There two others stood waiting in front of the house. They both held handguns.

"We found him coming up the road," one of his captors explained to the new guys. "He says he's Alex's friend, the dude from Honolulu."

"Okay," one guy said. "We'll take it from here. Go back to your posts." Then he waved his pistol toward the porch at the front of the house. "Let's go see Alex," he said to Bishop.

Bishop nodded and walked up the steps onto the porch and then to the front door with the two men following. One stepped in front of him, opened the door, and nodded to Bishop to enter. Once inside, they went down a hallway and then turned into a room that looked like a home office. Sitting behind the desk in the room with a smile on his face was Alex Baker. He stood up and walked around the desk with an outstretched hand. Bishop shook it.

"Rick, you found me," Baker said.

"Yeah, finally. Abby and I ran into a little trouble after arriving in Maui yesterday afternoon."

"Yes, I heard Kia betrayed me," Baker said. "I'm sorry for any inconvenience, bud. How did you get here?"

"A guy named Preston brought me."

"Ah, I thought as much."

"So, you called Abby from here and told her to bring me here to Maui to help get you out of a jam?"

"Well, I called her from the resort, but that's mostly right. She should have told you that. You're the only friend I had to turn to for help."

"I can believe that, considering all the trouble you've got me into."

"I'm sorry about that, Rick. But I expected you and Abby to arrive earlier. And then, the situation changed, and I had to come here when remaining at the resort became untenable. I wouldn't have asked you to come if I hadn't been in such a tough spot."

Bishop glanced around the room. "You call this a tough spot? You seem safe enough here to me."

"Sure, but I'm also a prisoner here, Rick. The road you came here on is the only way in and out, and my enemies control it. My friends here can hold them off, but I'm stuck here."

"Oh, so it's something of a Mexican stand-off."

"Exactly."

"All I know is that you put Abby and me in a tough spot yesterday."

"Yes, I know, and I'm sorry about that. Is she all right? I spoke to her on the phone, and she said she was okay. But it's hard to tell with Abby. She always puts up a brave front."

"Abby is fine for the time being," Bishop said. "Which brings me to the reason Preston brought me here. He told me to give you a message."

"What message?"

"It seems Abby's continued good health depends on you dividing the money with him and his guys, as originally agreed."

"Yes, well, you can go back to Preston and tell him I'll be in touch soon. I'll have someone drive you back."

"Sure, okay, Alex," Bishop said, nodding. Then he walked toward the door. The two men who had escorted him into the house stood on either side of the doorway.

"Hang on, Rick," Baker said. "You mean that's all you're willing to do for me?"

"That's right," Bishop said.

"All right. That's fine. I suppose I thought we were better friends than that. These guys will take you back to meet Preston."

"What else did you expect me to do, Alex? And what about Abby? I told you Preston threatened to harm her if you don't give them what they want."

"Trust me, Rick, Abby can take care of herself. She was a CIA officer in Afghanistan when we met. And Abby is tough as they come."

"With you as a friend, Alex, a person better keep their health insurance premiums paid up."

Bishop turned back to the door, and the two escorts turned to lead him out. Bishop reached around one guy and snatched the revolver from his waistband. He shoved the other guy against the wall. Then, holding the gun on them, Bishop said, "Don't move. Put your hands on the wall."

The two escorts did as he said, and Rick took the pistol from the other man's waistband.

"Now, turn around, Alex, and put your hands on the desk."

Baker didn't move for a moment, wondering if Bishop was serious. But deciding he was, he turned and put both palms on the desk.

Bishop crossed the room to Alex and tossed one pistol on the floor in a far corner of the room. Then he patted Alex down for a weapon but didn't find one. When he backed away, Alex turned to face him.

"You wouldn't shoot me, would you, Rick?" he said with a grin.

"If you want to test me, try something, Alex."

Bake's grin evaporated.

"Well, you're wasting your efforts if this chivalry is on Abby's behalf, I assure you."

"I'm doing this for myself," Bishop said, shoving Baker toward the door. "Let's go."

"Where?"

"Back to the resort."

"You're taking me to Preston?"

"No, to Craig Lynch, NCIS. He's following the money and looking for you, too. What happens after that is between you and the government."

Baker grinned. "So, you met Agent Lynch then?"

"Yes, and I know all about your heist of the $10 million from the government while you were in Kabul as a DOD contractor."

"You make it sound worse than it was, Rick."

"You're a thief, Alex. How do you expect me to make it sound noble?"

"Rick, you don't understand what it was like in Afghanistan then. Petraeus had introduced COIN, his counter-insurgency strategy. I'm sure you must have heard of it."

"Sure, I know what it was. So what does that have to do with you stealing government money?"

"Everything, Rick. They were handing out stacks of American dollars to goat herders barely out of the stone age, believing they were winning hearts and minds by buying loyalty. But most of that money was going right into the pockets of the Taliban warlords, who were using our own money to pay their fighters and buy more Russian weapons to kill Americans with. So, a few buds and I took a little of the money to keep it from being used for its intended corrupt purposes."

"Oh, well, that was noble," Bishop said sarcastically.

"Okay, sure, we took the money for ourselves, but at the same time, the Taliban didn't get it. So we saved American lives."

"That's only rationalization, Alex. But before we go, a question has occurred to me."

"What's that?"

"How exactly did you envision me helping you get away from Preston?"

"Well, I thought you and I could exchange identities."

Bishop gave Baker a baleful stare. "Alex, we look nothing alike."

"Yes, but it's you and I who know that."

"So does Mark Preston," Bishop said impatiently.

"Yes, but if he lost track of us here and discovered that Abby and a man left Maui together on a chartered flight to the mainland, naturally, he'd assume that man was Alex Baker. He would hardly expect me to return to Honolulu after he already found me there."

It all made sense to Bishop then. If he accompanied Abby on a charter flight to the mainland and they got away without Preston and his men actually seeing them, when Preston learned about it, he probably would assume it had been Alex on the flight. After all, that's how it had gone since the beginning. When Preston got close, Alex had taken off somewhere else, and the merry chase continued.

"Okay, I'll buy that, Alex. It might have worked. But you know, Preston is out there waiting on that road. Is there another way out of here?"

"No, but I figure my friends here can keep him pinned down long enough for us to get past him. Then we're home free."

"All right, Alex. Let's do it. But you make sure your friends understand they better not try anything stupid." Then Bishop thumbed back the hammer on the revolver and pointed it at Baker. "Or they will lose a wonderful friend. Roger that?"

"Oh, absolutely," Baker said.

CHAPTER NINE

The Great Escape

ALEX BAKER CLIMBED BEHIND the wheel of an open-topped Jeep, and Bishop got in the front seat beside him. Eight of Baker's friends with rifles climbed into the back of a beat-up Ford truck, and then, with the Ford in the lead, they took the dirt track back toward the clearing where Preston was waiting. The truck stopped about three hundred meters before reaching the clearing, and the armed men climbed out. Baker stopped the Jeep beside the truck.

"We'll wait here," Baker said. "Once they open up on Preston, we'll zip right past him and make our escape."

"They won't kill him, will they?" Bishop said.

"Oh no, I'd never ask them to do that. They will just pin him down and keep him away from his car until we're safely past."

Bishop watched the men fanning out into the trees. Then he noticed a pair of binoculars on the floorboard. Grabbing the binoculars, he put them to his eyes and could see the men spreading out, encircling the clearing on three sides. Bishop could also see Preston leaning against the front fender of his rental car, smoking a cigarette. Suddenly gunfire erupted from the trees. The first volley blew the windshield out of the car, and bullets punched holes in the car's steel body. Preston dived to the ground. Bullets peppered the dirt around him, but Bishop saw the shooters weren't trying to hit him. Still, he expected Preston didn't know that.

After several moments, Preston low-crawled around the car and took cover behind a dirt berm. Bullets poured into it, making Preston get and stay small.

"It's time to go," Baker said, slamming the Jeep into gear and mashing the gas. The Jeep rocketed forward and roared down the dirt road. As they approached Preston's car, the shooting stopped long enough for the Jeep to fly past and then erupted again. Bishop looked back and locked eyes with Preston for an instant as the Jeep shot past him.

"Think he got a good look at us?" Baker shouted.

"Yeah, he saw us," Bishop shouted back.

"Excellent. I love it when a plan comes together."

Baker kept the accelerator on the floor, and the Jeep shot down the road sending up a plume of dust in its wake. By the time Baker eased off the gas, Bishop realized the shooting had stopped.

"Unless they took out his car's radiator, Preston will be after us," Bishop shouted over the wind noise and roar of the engine. "They have stopped shooting."

"We have a good head start," Baker shouted back.

After about a mile, the Jeep careened around a bend in the road. Then Baker jammed on the brakes and slewed left. Two felled trees lay across the road ahead, with a dark sedan parked beyond them in the middle of the road. The Jeep skidded on the dirt, Baker lost control, and the Jeep went off the road into a shallow ditch. The front slammed into a dirt embankment, and the engine died. Bishop had barely braced for impact when they came to the sudden stop, and the collision nearly ejected him, causing the revolver to fly out of his hand into the brush.

Two men with handguns rushed up to the Jeep, the same two men Bishop had seen with Preston at the resort.

"Out of the Jeep," one said, brandishing his pistol.

"Move it," the other said.

With a hurried glance, Baker communicated something to Bishop only another former special operator would understand. Then they both started climbing out of the Jeep. Bishop pretended to stumble, which distracted the two men for an instant, and that was all Baker needed. He grabbed the gun side wrist of the man beside him and simultaneously delivered a palm strike beneath the point of the man's chin. Then, with a slick krav maga move, he stripped the man's weapon from his hand. Finally, pivoting behind the man and grabbing a fistful of his collar and jerking him off balance, Baker pointed the gun at the other man beside Bishop.

"Throw your gun into the weeds. Do it now."

The man beside Bishop hesitated only a second before tossing the weapon. Then Baker shoved the man he had disarmed toward his partner and Bishop.

"Everybody down on the ground, bellies in the dirt," Baker said.

Bishop took a step toward Baker as the two men went to the ground. Baker pointed the weapon at his chest.

"You too, bud," he said to Bishop. "Sorry, but I have to travel fast and light. So I don't need any company."

Bishop looked at him in disbelief, but seeing the look in Baker's eyes, Bishop joined the two men on the ground.

"Don't anyone get off the ground until I'm gone unless you want to get shot," Baker said. "I have hurt no one so far. Let's keep it that way."

Then Baker skirted the men on the ground and side-stepped toward the dark sedan on the other side of the downed trees. Seeing the keys in the ignition through the open passenger door window, he walked around and got in behind the wheel. After starting the car, he slewed it around with the tires spraying dirt and gravel and then drove away towards the highway.

Preston's men jumped up, and one ran to the weeds where he'd tossed his gun. Then Preston drove up and slammed on the brakes, stopping his car just short of the downed trees.

"What the hell happened?" Preston shouted as he jumped out of the car.

"Baker jumped me and got away," one man said. "He took our car."

"Damn it, get those trees out of the way and get in the car."

The two men hurried to the trees, dragged them to the side to clear the road, and then ran to Preston's car.

"What about him?" one said, pointing at Bishop.

"Forget him," Preston growled, getting behind the wheel. Then they slammed their car doors, and Preston's car rocketed away down the road.

Bishop stood in the middle of the road with his hands on his hips.

"Guess that means I don't get the other thousand," he said ruefully. Then he walked back to the Jeep to see if he could get it out of the ditch.

After looking it over, he saw the Jeep wasn't driveable. One of the front tires was flat, and the impact with the dirt bank had cracked the radiator, and all the coolant had leaked out onto the dry creek bed. Shrugging, he climbed the bank to the road and started walking toward the highway, hoping he could thumb a ride back to civilization when he got there.

CHAPTER TEN

Rescue Me

BISHOP HAD THE HIGHWAY in view when a low-flying helicopter flew past above him. When he looked up at it, he was sure it was Gabby Inouye's bird. The helicopter banked into a wide turn and then descended toward an open field to the right of the dirt road. Bishop jogged toward it, thinking Abby Stone had come to his rescue as it touched down. But when the door opened, it was Craig Lynch who jumped out instead of Abby. Lynch windmilled his arm, encouraging Bishop to hurry to the helicopter.

"Bishop, it looks like you ran into some trouble," Lynch said. "Need a lift?"

"What are you doing here?"

"Abigail Stone called my hotel room and told me I might find you out here. She arranged for me to use this helicopter. You seem upset?"

"Well, I'm sure I'll feel better when I see my old friends again."

"That helicopter pilot doesn't seem to like you much," Lynch said. "I thought I might have to force her to land at gunpoint to pick you up."

"Yeah, well, that's a long story," Bishop said. "Shall we get in the bird?"

"Of course."

Bishop climbed in back, and Lynch took his seat in front. Once they buckled in and Gabby had the bird airborne again, Lynch turned, tapped his headset, and pointed at something beside Bishop. When he looked that way, Bishop saw a headset hanging from a hook and put it on.

"Can you hear me?" Lynch said.

"Loud and clear."

"Good. What happened back there?"

"Preston and his guys had Baker bottled up at an old abandoned sugar cane plantation. We broke out, but Preston's guys were waiting for us with a roadblock. They stopped us, but Baker got the drop on them, and then he got away in their car and left me behind."

Lynch chuckled. "What a guy, huh? But we must give the devil his due. Alex Baker is a resourceful, slippery man."

"Hey, look there," Bishop said, pointing at the ground. "That's Preston's car now."

"I'm not concerned about them at the moment. It's Baker I want."

Bishop nodded and continued looking out the window at the ground. Then, a few minutes later, he pointed at the ground again.

"Lynch, that's the car Baker was driving. I wonder why he stopped? Preston isn't far behind him."

"Land down there," Lynch said to Gabby.

Gabby nodded and descended toward the field next to the highway and near the car. Once Gabby landed, Lynch and Bishop jumped out and jogged toward the car on the shoulder. Alex Baker got out, wearing a sheepish grin.

"It ran out of gas," he shouted.

"Come on, Alex," Bishop shouted back. "Get in the bird. Preston will be here any minute."

Baker nodded and jogged toward the helicopter, but he stopped when he saw Lynch pointing a semi-automatic at him.

"Hands on top of your head, Baker," Lynch said. "And don't move. Bishop told me what happened, and I know you have a weapon."

After Baker put his hands on his head, Lynch walked over, frisked him, and took the gun from Baker's waistband.

"Now you can get in the bird," he said to Baker.

Bishop followed them, but Lynch turned and pointed his gun at him.

"Sorry, Bishop, not you. I can't take you while transporting a prisoner."

"Come on, Lynch. You must be kidding."

"No, sorry, I'm not. Some good Samaritan will probably stop and give you a lift. Just keep your thumb out."

Then, after a chuckle, Lynch followed Baker into the helicopter. Bishop looked at Gabby through the windscreen. She made a pouty face at him and then smiled. Then the bird lifted off and flew away.

A minute later, Preston's car drove up. Preston looked into the car Baker had left on the side of the highway, over at the front seat passenger, shaking his head, and then he punched the accelerator, and the car sped away. They hadn't even glanced at Bishop.

Bishop sighed, loosened his tie, and started walking west along the shoulder of the highway, whistling the old Louis Armstrong number, *Nobody Knows the Trouble I've Seen*.

Bishop had walked for almost two hours, but was still miles from the coast where the highway turned from west to north. Only three cars had passed him since Lynch left him stranded. Unfortunately, all three had been driving east. He hoped he'd have more luck once he made it to the coast, but that would be late into the afternoon at his rate of travel. He expected his chances of hitching a ride would decrease even further if he were still walking when the sun went down in the evening.

In the distance, he saw another eastbound car approaching, which did him no good. He kept walking west without bothering to look at the car as it passed. But then he heard the pitch of the engine change and realized the car was slowing. He looked back over his shoulder to see the driver making a U-turn on the deserted stretch of highway. And then the car came back toward him. The driver slowly passed him and then pulled to the shoulder ahead and stopped. Bishop figured it must be a kind soul stopping to see if he needed help. He jogged to the car's passenger side as the driver lowered the window.

When Bishop leaned in the window to speak to the driver, it delighted him to discover a smiling Abby Stone sitting behind the wheel.

"Need a lift, sailor?" she chuckled.

"I sure do," Bishop said with a grin. He opened the door and slid into the front passenger seat.

"Well, for a place as deserted as the moon, you sure run into a lot of people you know out here," he said.

"I sent a man named Craig Lynch to look for you this morning in the helicopter I chartered. But when I heard nothing from him, I drove down to look for you myself. He didn't find you?"

"He found me all right," Bishop said. "But when we came across cousin Alex and landed to pick him up, Lynch booted me off the flight at gunpoint and left me stranded out here in the boonies."

"I was afraid something like that had happened," Stone said, putting the car in gear and pulling back onto the highway. "So Alex is with Lynch?"

"That's right. Why do I get the impression you sent Lynch to look for good old cousin Alex, not me?"

"Look, Rick, I've meant to talk to you about that. Alex isn't really my cousin."

"Well, you could have fooled me," Bishop said, not bothering to hide the sarcasm.

"Alex is a good friend. So, yes, I asked Lynch to look for him, but you as well. I've grown very fond of you since we met, Rick."

"So, what's the story with you and Alex?"

"Alex got into some trouble a few years ago. He stole some money. Well, a lot of money. You don't know what he's been through, Rick. Those men have hounded him almost all over the world. He'd like to give the money back and stop the running, but he doesn't want to go to federal prison."

"Well, that's certainly understandable."

"I was hoping you could talk Alex into telling you where the money is. Then he and I could get away, and you and Lynch could share the reward. Do you think Lynch would agree to that?"

"I think Agent Lynch intends to put Alex in federal prison," Bishop said, "even if he recovers the money. And I don't expect he plans to cut me in on any reward."

"He can't!" Abby exclaimed.

"Well, he's doing it," Bishop said. "He has already arrested Alex, and that helicopter with Alex and Lynch aboard should be back at the airport by now."

"No, it isn't," Abby said, grinning at Bishop.

"You trying to tell me something?"

"I chartered the helicopter and am paying the pilot, so I suppose I have something to say about where it lands."

"And that's not Kapalua Airport?"

"It is not."

"Gabby will fly them around for a while. I paid her for two hours. Then she will land where I told her, and we'll already be there waiting."

"Well, I think nothing about this deal would surprise me anymore," Bishop said. "And while I'd like to have a little chat with Lynch myself, I will not help Alex escape from federal custody. I don't have any desire to go to federal prison either."

"Don't worry, Rick. No one will ask you to do anything illegal."

CHAPTER ELEVEN

The Rendezvous

ABOUT TWENTY-FIVE MINUTES AFTER picking Bishop up, Abby turned off the highway and drove up to a small house overlooking the beach.

"What's this place?" Bishop said when Abby turned off the car and prepared to get out.

"It's a vacation rental that I picked up the key to this morning," Abby said. "And this is where Gabby will land shortly."

Bishop followed Abby into the house after she unlocked the door.

"There are sandwiches and beer in the fridge if you're hungry, Rick."

"I'd love some sandwiches and beer," Bishop said. "As soon as I get some water. I'm dying of thirst after my long walk."

Abby laughed. "Well, there is also plenty of bottled water in the frig."

While Bishop drank his fill of water, Abby set a platter of sandwiches out on the kitchen bar with a large container of macaroni salad. Then she found some paper plates and plastic utensils in a cabinet. Bishop took a plate and eyed the sandwiches.

"Try one of the ham salad ones," Abby said. "Only they make the sandwiches with Spam instead of ham. It seems the people of Hawaii truly love their Spam."

"That's no surprise," Bishop said. "Spam is about all the people in Hawaii had to eat during World War Two. And even after the war ended, they still loved the Spam."

"That explains it then."

Bishop selected two sandwiches, dipped himself a heaping portion of macaroni salad, and opened a can of beer. Then they heard a car drive up out front.

"I thought you said Gabby was bringing them in the helicopter," Bishop said.

"That was the plan," Abby said. "Something must have gone wrong." She got up from the bar and walked toward the front door.

It opened before Stone made it to the door, and Mark Preston strode in triumphantly with his two pals. All three held guns in their hands. Bishop stood up.

"Well, if it isn't Bishop," Preston said. "Sit back down, Bishop, unless you want the lady to get hurt."

Bishop sat back down on the stool at the bar.

"And you can join him, sweetheart," Preston said to Abby. Then he turned to one of his men. "Go get the car out of sight. I expect Alex will make an appearance soon."

The man nodded and went back out the front door.

"My, that was thoughtful of you to prepare lunch for us, Abigail," Preston said, grabbing a sandwich off the platter. "I'm starving."

"How did you find us?" Abby said.

"We saw you on the highway after we lost Alex, and we followed you here." Preston's man came back inside after hiding their car. "You boys have some lunch. You were complaining about being hungry."

The two men helped themselves to sandwiches and beers. Preston grabbed a beer and sat down at the end of the bar, holding his gun casually in his other hand, pointed toward Bishop and Stone.

"Yeah, we'll enjoy lunch with Abigail and her friend Bishop and see what develops," he said.

"We should have arrived at the airport over an hour ago," Lynch said impatiently to Gabby Inouye, speaking into the mic of his headset.

"It must be an electrical short," Inouye retorted. "First, the GPS stopped working and now the radio. And I'm not familiar with this part of Maui, so I got disoriented. I think I know where we are now, but I'm going to have to set the bird down."

"Land out here? Why?"

"Because I'm losing hydraulic pressure. If it falls to zero, so will we."

Alex Baker sat in the rear compartment, unable to hear what the pilot and Lynch were talking about, since no one had offered him a headset. But he could guess. He sat quietly with a knowing smile on his lips.

Gabby found a spot to land that satisfied her, and she put the helicopter down on a flat area atop a ridge line next to the coast. After the skids touched down, she shut down the bird.

"What are you going to do?"

"Troubleshoot the hydraulic system," she said, unbuckling and getting out.

Lynch sighed and got out, too. He opened the rear door.

"You might as well get out and stretch your legs," he said to Baker. "We may be here for a while. There is something wrong with the helicopter."

Baker nodded and got out. Gabby had an access panel removed and was checking the hydraulic lines.

"Find the problem?" Lynch said.

"There is a leak in a hydraulic line," she said without looking back at him. "The line must have rubbed against something from the vibration until it developed a leak."

"Can you fix it?"

"I can fix the line temporarily until we get back to the airport, where I can replace it. But the hydraulic fluid is low. I can't fly until I top off the reservoir."

"Where are we going to get hydraulic fluid out here?"

"We aren't," Gabby said. "I'll have to get someone at the airport to bring some out. But the radio isn't working, and there's no cellular signal out here."

Lynch retrieved his mobile from his jacket pocket. "Damn, I have no signal either."

Gabby shielded her eyes from the sun and looked around. Then she pointed to a small house below the ridge on the beach.

"While I repair the hydraulic leak, why don't you guys walk down to the house there and see if they have a landline you can use? Then you can call the airport and ask them to send someone out here with ten gallons of hydraulic fluid for a McDonnell Douglas 500E."

"Call who at the airport?" Lynch said.

"Just ask for aviation maintenance and support. Whoever answers will be able to help."

"And tell them to bring it where?" Lynch said. "You said we're lost."

"Get the address from the residents at the house. Jeez Louise, Lynch. It's not rocket science."

"If there is anyone at home," Lynch said.

"I saw a car in front and one behind those trees beside the house when I was looking for a landing site," Gabby said. "With two vehicles there, I'm sure someone must be at home. So, get going."

Gabby turned and went back to work inside the maintenance compartment.

Lynch muttered something under his breath and then turned to Baker. "Come on, Baker, you're going with me. I'm not letting you out of my sight."

"Whatever you say, Lynch. I'm up for a little walk."

Lynch went back to the cockpit and opened the passenger door. Then he reached in and pulled the key from the ignition and pocketed it. He wasn't sure he trusted the pilot. Maybe there was nothing wrong with the helicopter, and she planned to leave them here for some reason. But without the key, she wouldn't go anywhere. The two men started downhill towards the house.

Gabby, unaware that Lynch had taken the key to the bird, turned and watched the men go. Then she replaced the access panel with a grin. After tightening the screws, she wiped her hands with a shop rag. Then she sat down on the ground with her back against a skid support and made herself comfortable. Abigail Stone had told her to wait after landing until she saw the car in front of the house drive away.

CHAPTER TWELVE

The Double-Cross

SOMEONE KNOCKED ON THE front door, and Preston told Bishop to answer it. Bishop got to his feet, snagging an unopened beer off the bar. Crossing the room, he held the beer can next to his leg, surreptitiously shaking the contents by rotating his wrist back and forth. Preston's accomplices took up positions beside the door with their guns out.

When Bishop opened the door, Alex Baker burst in with a broad smile, with Lynch following behind him. But Baker's smile became a frown when he saw Preston standing next to the bar with a gun in his hand.

"Alex, darling, there has been an unexpected change of plans," Stone said.

"Alex," Preston said. "You finally arrived. We've just been having lunch while we waited."

One of Preston's cohorts shoved Lynch face-first against the wall, patted him down, and reached into Lynch's jacket to take the pistol from his shoulder holster.

The other henchman watched his partner disarming Lynch, and Bishop made the most of the momentary distraction. Slipping a finger beneath the beer can tab, he aimed the top of the can at the inattentive guy's face and popped it, sending a stream of agitated beer into the man's eyes. Then he ripped the pistol from the hand of the temporarily blinded thug.

Simultaneously, almost as if they had choreographed it, Baker attacked the second thug still occupied with Lynch and took both the man's handgun and the weapon he'd just taken from Lynch. Preston's reaction to the unfolding melee was far too slow. By the time he brought his gun up, Stone, who had jumped to her feet and lifted her stool above her head, smashed it down on top of Preston's head, knocking him senseless. His dropped handgun skittered across the floor, and Stone hastily scooped it up. The three bad guys were down, and Bishop, Baker, and Stone all held pistols.

"There is only one problem, Alex," Bishop said. "Lynch already arrested you, and I won't help you escape from federal custody. Your shenanigans have already caused me enough trouble, and I'm not going to federal prison for you."

Baker chuckled. "Rick, I know Lynch told you he is an NCIS agent, but it's a lie. First, his name isn't Craig Lynch. Allow me to introduce you to the former Petty Officer First Class Brian Greenwood. Brian was a logistics specialist in Kabul, who helped us smuggle the money out of Afghanistan."

"But he showed me NCIS credentials," Bishop said.

"Which are fake or stolen, I assure you. Even though we paid Brian well for his services, after NCIS arrested him for an unrelated offense, he identified all of us to them as part of a plea bargain. But he still spent five years in Leavenworth. And ever since they paroled him, he has been after me to get part of the money after he learned I had all of it."

"That begs another question," Bishop said. "Why so greedy? It seems $10 million should be enough to go around. So why did you cut out your three partners and keep all the money? It seems if everyone had gotten their $2.5 million cuts, you would have saved yourself a lot of grief."

"Cut them out? They planned to cut me out. I never really trusted any of them, so I left a hidden voice-activated micro-recorder in the house we stayed in whenever I went out alone. One evening, when I returned and checked it, I heard them discussing their plan to turn me into the feds and split my share. So, I went to the port in Long Beach a day early, made my own deal with our contact there, and then absconded with all the money."

"I'm shocked," Bishop said. "Is there no honor among thieves anymore?"

Baker laughed. "It appears not."

"Well, since I'm not helping you escape federal custody, Alex, I'll keep these gentlemen occupied while you and Abby bring the car around."

"Great idea, Rick. Come outside when you hear me honk."

Baker and Stone went out the front door.

Preston's cohorts had joined him after getting off the floor and had Preston sitting up on the floor, regaining his senses.

Bishop pointed his gun at Greenwood. "Get over there with the others, Agent Lynch," he said. "Unfortunately, we won't have room for you in the car."

Sullenly Greenwood joined the unhappy band of criminals. Not that Bishop wasn't preparing to leave with a criminal himself. Bishop gave the men his parting words when he heard the car horn sound outside.

"Anyone who sticks his head out the door before we're gone gets a bullet," he said. He then backed to the door and went out, closing the door behind him.

As soon as he stepped outside, Bishop felt a gun pressed against his back.

"I'm so sorry, Rick darling, but give me the gun," Abby said.

"You plan to shoot me, Abby?"

"I will if I must, but I'd truly hate to end a beautiful friendship with a bullet. I'm very fond of you, Rick. But half of $10 million is $5 million. And $5 million is $5 million."

Bishop half-turned and handed the gun to Abby.

"I guess it's true," Bishop said.

"What's that?"

"A greedy woman is a greedy woman."

Abby smiled, backing away toward the car. "Goodbye, Rick."

Bishop nodded. Then he looked at Alex Baker behind the wheel of Abby's rental.

"Rick, you'll hear from me, bud," he shouted out the open car window. "I promise I'll get a certified check in the mail to you for services rendered at the first opportunity."

"Save it, Alex," Rick shouted back. "You'll need your money for a good lawyer."

Baker smiled broadly, and then he and Abby Stone drove away.

When Bishop turned and looked at the front door of the house, it occurred to him that four angry criminals would burst out of it at any moment. And he no longer had a gun. So, he sprinted to the opposite side of the house from the trees he'd seen Preston's guy had concealed their car behind.

He had barely hidden himself when the door banged open, and Preston and his two associates rushed outside and then to their car when they saw the other car was gone. They jumped in the car and sped down the driveway toward the highway. Bishop guessed they hadn't had room for Lynch either, and the fake NCIS agent was still inside the house.

Cautiously, Bishop entered the house, where he found the man sitting at the bar eating a sandwich and drinking beer.

"Might as well join me, Bishop," he said. "There is still plenty of food and beer left."

Under the circumstances, Bishop thought that was decent of the man, so he joined him at the bar and opened a beer.

"Well, here we are again, Lynch."

"No hard feelings, I hope, Bishop. I'm sorry for marooning you out in the middle of nowhere, but I couldn't take any chances. And then you tried to do the same to me. So, the way I see it, we're even."

Bishop nodded. "No hard feelings."

Greenwood held up his beer, and Bishop bumped it with his can in a toast.

"I suppose everything Alex Baker said was true?" Bishop said. "You aren't an NCIS agent named Lynch?"

"Yes, sadly, all true," the man said. "Let's begin again. I'm Brian Greenwood. Pleased to meet you."

"Thanks. So how much did you get for helping them with the caper in Afghanistan, Brian? If you don't mind me asking."

"Ten thousand. But when NCIS busted me on the other thing, I had to turn it over with the rest of my ill-gotten gains as part of the sentence reduction deal."

"So that's why you were trying to get something back from Alex?"

"Yeah, it seemed my best option when they paroled me. I came out of Leavenworth with no Navy career, no money, and no prospects as a convicted felon with a dishonorable discharge. But I knew a guy in Leavenworth who knew one guy in the robbery crew. He'd heard Baker took the whole $10 million and told me about it. So, I figured if I tracked him down, I might extort some of the money out of him by threatening to dime him out to the feds or his former partners."

"But he wouldn't go for it?"

"Well, every time I found him, he agreed to pay me off, but then he'd skip town, and I had to find him all over again. I thought I had him this time when I found him in Honolulu. Then I let him sucker me into walking into that closet you freed me from."

"Alex ever mention where the money was?"

"No, Alex is greedy and untrustworthy, but he's no fool. I doubt the woman even knows."

"So, what are you going to do now? Continue the chase?"

"No, I'm giving it up. I can't afford to continue it, anyway. No telling where Alex will go from here."

"He must have the money hidden somewhere," Bishop said. "He couldn't risk parking in a bank, not even in a safe deposit box somewhere. If so, he might not be able to get to it when he had to leave someplace in a hurry."

"Yeah, I expect you're right. But, anyway, I don't even have the money to get back to the mainland right now. So, I guess I'll have to find whatever work I can here in Hawaii if I want to eat. Who knows? Maybe I'll stay. Hawaii doesn't seem a terrible place to live. At least the weather is nice if you have to live on the street."

"So, do you regret getting into all the shady stuff that has cost you everything you had?"

"Well, hindsight is always 20/20, buddy. But you know something? I didn't feel like a crook in Afghanistan. The government was pouring cash into the country like it was the water over Niagara Falls, and they were wasting all of it. They were bribing officials who were already corrupt enough without our help. They spent over $5 million putting in a freaking gender studies program for the

Afghans. Can you believe it? I bet the Taliban are still laughing their asses off about how stupid Americans are. Everyone I knew in the military was making money on the side. So, after a while, I felt like a chump for not getting my part of the action. But it was so easy to do, you couldn't stop yourself from getting greedy. And that's why they caught me. So, being honest about it, I'm damn sorry I got caught. But that's about it."

"Yeah, considering the circumstances, I suppose I can understand it," Bishop said. "Well, I guess we'll have to hitchhike back to Lahaina. They left with all the cars."

"Not necessarily," Greenwood said, removing a key ring from his pocket and dangling it in front of Bishop.

"What's that?"

"The key to the helicopter that brought us here. The pilot landed, claiming she was having hydraulic problems. But I suspected she was lying. And being the suspicious type, I took the key before Alex and I walked down to this house. I'm sure it's still up there on the ridge where we landed."

"That's great news, Greenwood," Bishop said. "Let's go find out."

Chapter Thirteen

Back to Lahaina

A VISIBLY INCENSED GABBY Inouye stood leaning against her bird, glaring at Bishop and Greenwood as they trudged uphill.

"You had no right taking my key," she said to Greenwood.

"I took it because I knew you were lying," Greenwood said. "You lied about the hydraulic problem. You lied about the electrical short. And I'm sure now you even lied about being lost."

"I didn't owe you anything, Lynch. I only followed the instructions of the people paying me. Now give me back my damn key."

Greenwood tossed the key to her. Bishop saw no reason to get into a discussion about Greenwood being Greenwood, not Lynch. It was a long story, and he was tired. He only wanted to get back to Lahaina and then Honolulu after getting some rest.

"Thanks for nothing," Gabby said to Greenwood. "Now, you two can get the hell away from my bird."

"Come on, Gabby," Bishop pleaded. "You're going back to Lahaina anyway. Can't we ride along?"

"No, not even if you offered to pay, which I'm sure you won't."

"Speaking of that," Bishop said. "I hope you got most of what Abby Stone agreed to pay you. She and Alex Baker split in her car, and I'm sure you will never see or hear from her again."

"What!" Gabby exclaimed. "Are you kidding me? She hasn't paid me anything except for the original charter before we left Honolulu. So she owes me for an overnight and the little ruse she asked for this morning."

"Yeah, well, as I've learned, neither she nor her boyfriend, Alex, can be trusted as far as you could throw them."

"Damn it," Gabby said. "They're your friends, so I should have known. I should never have agreed to fly you two to Maui, much less to the extras."

"So, can we get a ride back? We're stuck here otherwise."

"No, Bishop, you can't."

Greenwood pulled out his fake NCIS credentials. "Ms. Inouye, you lied to a federal agent, and now you're interfering with a federal investigation. I suggest you rethink your position unless you're eager to spend some time in a federal lockup."

"Suddenly, seeing the look of concern on Gabby's face, Bishop was very happy he hadn't corrected her when she had addressed Greenwood as Lynch."

"Is the government going to reimburse me?" Gabby said stubbornly, never one to accept defeat gracefully.

"I'll submit a request, but I can't guarantee my supervisor will approve it after the fact," Greenwood said. "But I promise you this. If you leave us stranded, it will be the last flying you will do for a long while."

"Why do I have to take him?" Gabby whined, pointing her finger at Bishop. "He's not a federal agent. He's barely a human being."

"Mr. Bishop is a material witness in an important federal criminal investigation with national security ramifications. Therefore, I need to debrief him without delay."

Gabby sighed. "Fine. I'll warm up the bird."

She turned, walked around the helicopter, and got in. Soon the engine started, and the rotors turned slowly.

"Well done, Brian," Bishop said. "You almost had me convinced."

"Well, she lied to me, so I see no reason I can't lie to her."

"Sure, I get it," Bishop said. "But a word to the wise. She isn't a woman whose bad side you want to get on. And when she finds out she isn't getting paid by the government, you will be on her bad side."

"Like you, Bishop?"

"Exactly."

A few minutes later, Gabby gestured to them to get in. Greenwood got in the front passenger seat, and Bishop got in the back. This time he didn't care. It sure beat hoofing it all the way back to Lahaina.

On the flight back, Gabby didn't say a word to Bishop or Greenwood. And when they talked with each other over the headsets, Gabby flipped the intercom function on her headset off so she wouldn't even have to listen to them.

"So, are you going to look for Alex and Abigail?" Greenwood asked Bishop. "I'm only curious because I never understood why you got involved in this anyway."

"Well, I got involved because Alex and I have been friends a long time, and he told me he was in trouble. I just didn't know the trouble was with the three guys who helped him steal $10 million from the government and that he cut them out of their shares. Had I known that I wouldn't have agreed to help him."

"So you're out of it?"

"Well, I was working for Alex, so I don't have a client now. But, on the other hand, he will not pay me for services rendered. So I'd like to find a way to recoup my losses."

"You might not agree, but I think he owes them," Greenwood said. "I mean, they all took the same risks. It doesn't seem fair Alex gets to keep all the money."

"I can't disagree, even if what Alex said about them trying to cut him out was true. If he keeps the money, they should probably all get their shares. But it is stolen and should go back to the government. None of them should get any of it."

"You know, the Treasury Department pays rewards to people who help the government recover stolen money," Greenwood said. "If you could figure out where Alex hid it and got your hands on it, you could earn a substantial reward."

"Define substantial."

"I've heard ten to thirty percent, depending on the amount the government recovers and the circumstances."

"Jeez, even ten percent would be $1 million," Bishop said. "Maybe I will look for it. But first, I want to talk to some people I know."

"Yeah, a million isn't chump change," Greenwood said.

"You have any idea how hard it would be to move $10 million around?"

"Well, it would depend on what you used to carry it," Greenwood said. "A large gym bag, for example, would hold about a million. So Alex would need ten of those. But say he used a military-style duffle bag. It would hold two million easily. But that's about forty-five pounds. So I doubt he'd go much larger, and using bags like that, he'd still need five of them."

"Okay, that gives me some idea of the size of place he'd need to store that much cash."

"That closet in his office would have been perfect," Greenwood said. "I couldn't believe it when I found out that wasn't where he kept it."

"I don't think he'd leave it in his office," Bishop said. "I might try to find out where he lived in Honolulu. I think his residence would be a better bet."

"Unless he just buried it somewhere."

"I can't imagine that," Bishop said. "Would you risk burying $10 million where someone might stumble over it?"

"You're probably right. Maybe it is hidden wherever Alex lived."

Bishop thought about potential hiding places for a while. He racked his brain for anything Alex might have said that could be a clue to the money's whereabouts. But nothing came to mind.

"I guess I'll have to look for a homeless shelter or something when I get back to Honolulu," Greenwood said. "I'm broke. I paid for the room at that resort through the end of tonight, but I'll officially be homeless at check-out time in the morning."

"That will be tough," Bishop said. "There are tons of homeless people in Honolulu. There aren't enough shelters, so many live in tents and such in public areas."

"I don't suppose you could put me up for a few days until I find work?"

"No, my girlfriend lives with me, and I only have a small apartment," Bishop said.

"Sure, I understand. It's not like you owe me anything anyway. I shouldn't have put you on the spot like that."

Despite himself, Bishop felt sympathy for Greenwood. Sure he had made some mistakes, but he didn't seem like a bad guy.

"If you're desperate, I could let you bunk in my office for a few days," Bishop said. "I've got a cot and a sleeping bag. But you would have to be out and about during my work hours. And you can't let my landlady find out you are staying there."

"I am desperate, man," Greenwood said. "And that sounds a lot better than a homeless shelter. So I'd appreciate it, and I'll follow any rules you set."

"Okay, it's only a short-term fix," Bishop said. "But I know a few people I could talk to about giving you a job."

"You don't know how much I'd appreciate that, Rick. Unfortunately, I know no one in Honolulu, and well, with my record, I doubt I'll have an easy time finding anyone to hire me."

"Okay, we'll work on it when we get back."

"Jeez, it just occurred to me I don't have the money even to get back to Honolulu," Greenwood said.

Bishop leaned forward to make sure Gabby still had her intercom function turned off. Then, satisfied she wasn't listening, he said, "Yeah, don't worry about it. I'm pretty sure I can talk Gabby into giving us a ride back. But I don't think we should push our luck with the federal agent thing."

Greenwood chuckled. "Yeah, after seeing how she is, I'm already a little worried about how far I pushed it already."

Chapter Fourteen

Lodging Difficulties

Bishop had mixed feelings about the offer he'd made to help Greenwood. After all, he really knew nothing about Brian. But he felt sympathy for the man's tough situation. He supposed it wouldn't hurt to help him on a trial basis to see how things went. And he had already made the offer, and Brian had accepted. So, Rick figured he owed him that much.

Gabby put the bird down at Kapalua Airport. Then, after shutting everything down, she said, "Okay, I brought you both back, and that's the end of it. There is no reason for us to see each other again."

Turning to Greenwood, she continued, "Unless you get the approval to pay me. Then I want the check. And I expect you to do your best to make that happen."

"No promises, but I will do my best," Greenwood said solemnly in his most authoritative fake federal agent voice.

"Any chance we could hitch a ride back to Honolulu with you in the morning?" Bishop said.

"Bishop, what did you fail to understand about there is no reason for us ever seeing each other again. You absolutely may not ride back to Honolulu with me."

"Come on, Gabby. What would it hurt? I'll even chip in for fuel. You'll have to eat the fuel bill for today. It would cover some of your loss."

"I hate your guts, Bishop. I wouldn't take a penny from you if I were starving to death, and I never want you inside my bird again. Is that clear enough for you?"

"Well, just think it over, Gabby. You might change your mind after you sleep on it. And since Abigail paid for your rental car, can you give us a ride to the resort?"

Gabby covered her ears and screamed as loud as she could.

"I guess that's a no," Greenwood said, opening the door and climbing out of the helicopter.

Bishop got out, and he and Greenwood walked across the tarmac to the terminal.

"I thought you said you could talk her into giving us a lift back to Honolulu," Greenwood said.

"I'm not giving up yet," Bishop said. "That was just an opening salvo to soften her up. I'll find her at the hotel and keep working it."

"Yeah, good luck with that," Greenwood said. "I thought people only hated Trump the way that woman hates you."

"Come on," Bishop said. "I'll get us a taxi to the resort."

There were no taxis outside the terminal, so Bishop had to call for one. While he and Greenwood stood on the sidewalk waiting, Gabby walked up.

"Did you change your mind about giving us a ride?" Bishop asked in surprise.

"That bitch canceled my rental," Gabby said. "The car was missing from where I left it. So I went to the counter, and they told me the party paying for the rental called and told them to cancel and for them to pick up the car from the terminal."

"That sucks," Greenwood said. "So you waiting for a cab, too?"

Gabby looked at Bishop and twisted her lips into something she probably thought was a smile.

"I hate to ask, but I'm a little short on cash and don't have a credit card with me. Any chance I could ride to the resort with you guys? They charge the same rate for up to four passengers."

"Huh?" Bishop said. "I thought you never wanted to see me again? You sure you're up for being stuck inside a taxi with me all the way back to the resort?"

"Don't be a jerk about it, Bishop. Yes or no? Can I ride with you guys or not?"

"Mi el rodar de suelo, su el rodar de suelo," Bishop said.

Greenwood looked at Gabby. "That means—"

"I know what it means, Lynch! I speak fluent conversational Spanish."

Turning to Bishop, she said. "Thanks. It's the least you can do, considering."

"Honey, let's not fight," Bishop said.

Gabby rolled her eyes and turned to face the street.

The taxi arrived, and Gabby got into the front seat beside the driver. Bishop and Greenwood got in the back. Bishop paid the fare when the driver pulled up at the hotel, and the three walked into the lobby. Then they went their separate ways.

When Bishop got to his room, he inserted the key card in the slot, but the light on the card reader flashed red, and the door remained locked. After trying the card several times with the same result, Bishop assumed the card wasn't working and took the elevator back to the lobby. Gabby was at the front desk jawing at the clerk when he got there.

"But it's my room and it's paid for through tonight," Gabby said.

"I'm sorry, ma'am. As I explained, the guest who registered the room called and canceled. We've already refunded the charge for tonight to her credit card."

"But my luggage is still in that room."

"Let me check something," the clerk said. "Yes, the room is vacant. House-keeping hasn't cleaned it yet, so I can have someone go up and get your luggage for you. Or you can rent the room for the same rate as last night."

"Is there a problem?" Bishop said.

Gabby turned to face him. "Stone canceled my hotel room, too!" she exclaimed. "And I don't have a credit card with me."

"Oh, no wonder my card key didn't work," Bishop said. "She must have canceled mine, too."

"Which room, sir?" the clerk asked.

Bishop gave him the room number printed on the folder with his key card inside.

"Yes, sir," the clerk said, looking up from the computer terminal. "The same guest canceled that one as well."

"Okay," Bishop said. "Then I want to rent it for the night, and I'll pay with my debit card."

"That's fine, sir," the clerk said, taking Bishop's debit card.

Gabby pinched her nose, looked up at the ceiling, then closed her eyes for a moment. After taking a deep breath, she opened her eyes and looked at Bishop.

"You already know my circumstances. Could I impose on you to pay for my room for the night? I'll pay you back as soon as we get back to Honolulu."

"Jeez, I'd like to help you out, Gabby. But I'm sure I don't have enough in my account to put two rooms on my debit card." Then Bishop turned back to the clerk. "Is that room a double? I didn't stay there last night. I stayed elsewhere."

"Yes, sir, it is."

"There you go," Bishop said to Gabby. "As long as you promise to behave, you're welcome to bunk in my room. I only need one bed."

"You're such a jerk, Bishop. I hate your guts. I'll sleep outside on the beach before I'd stay in the same hotel room with you."

"Hm, well, how about this?" Bishop said. "If you give Lynch and me a ride back to Honolulu, I'll give you some fuel money, and you can pay for your room with that. Unfortunately, I'm short on cash too, but I'll go up to Lynch's room and borrow some cash from him."

Bishop had plenty of money in his bank account for once in his life. And Greenwood was broke. But if Gabby accepted the offer, he could pretend to borrow the money and then get it from the ATM he'd seen near the hotel bar entrance.

"I see what you're doing," Gabby said, "and the answer is still no. I'm not taking you guys back to Honolulu. No way."

"Well, that leaves us at an impasse, doesn't it? So unless you really plan to sleep on the beach, maybe Lynch will loan you the money for a room."

The clerk cleared his throat. "Excuse me, ma'am, but sleeping on the beach isn't allowed. It's against hotel policy and there is a county ordinance."

Gabby looked like she was going to scream again. Bishop steeled himself for it. He could tell she was taking deep breaths through her nose and exhaling through her mouth.

"Could my friend sleep in a chair here in the lobby?" Bishop asked the clerk. "Just for the evening?"

"No, sir, our facilities are only for registered guests."

"All right, Bishop, since you insist on being a jerk, I'll stay in your room. But don't you dare speak to me. You understand?"

"Hm, well, since you refuse to let us hitch a ride back to Honolulu with you, a trip you're making anyway, I'm not sure I see a good reason to subject myself to your hostility. Sure, I have an extra bed available, but I see now having you in my room would be very unpleasant for both of us."

"I can't believe you're stooping to blackmail. That's a new low even for you, and I didn't think you could go any lower."

"Okay," Bishop said. "I don't think we're getting anywhere, so enjoy your evening and have a nice flight back to Honolulu tomorrow."

Then Bishop took his new key card from the clerk and turned to walk to the elevator.

"All right!" Gabby exclaimed. "You can ride back, and I'll stay in your room. But I want a hundred and sixty for fuel."

Bishop suppressed a grin before he turned back to Gabby. Then, looking at the desk clerk, he said, "Could you have someone retrieve my friend's luggage from the room she stayed in last night and bring it to my room?"

"Yes, sir, right away."

Chapter Fifteen

Roomies

Rick Bishop was a simple man who preferred contemplating simple concepts. That's why he had dismissed the complex and unpleasant discussion with the hostile Gabby Inouye at almost the moment they boarded the elevator. He had needed a ride back to Honolulu. Gabby had to fly back there anyway, so Bishop had secured a ride back with her as best he could. He had solved the problem, and his thoughts turned to a more pleasant, simple concept, the most interesting point from his conversation with Greenwood. That was that the government paid a reward of between ten and thirty percent to anyone who helped them recover stolen government assets. Bishop figured he would never be in as good a position to get one million dollars all at one time as he was now with this opportunity.

Like most people, Bishop had often dreamed of having a million bucks. And a million bucks all at once, not earning that aggregate amount piecemeal after a lifetime of slaving away at work. So if he could find the stolen money Alex Baker had hidden and collected a $1 million check from Uncle Sam, Rick Bishop would be a millionaire, at least for one moment in time. Bishop enjoyed thinking about it so much that it annoyed him when Gabby jarred him back to the present when she carped at him before they even arrived on their floor.

"I sure hope you enjoyed humiliating me in front of the desk clerk," Gabby seethed.

"What are you talking about, Gabby?" Bishop said. "I did no such thing."

"Ha. Is it possible for my friend to sleep in a chair in the lobby for the night? What was that if not purposeful humiliation? You made me sound like a homeless bag lady."

The elevator doors opened, and the pair walked down the corridor to Bishop's hotel room.

"I was only seeking a creative solution to your problem of having nowhere to spend the night safely," Bishop said. "Which became necessary because you were argumentative and entirely non receptive to any of the other helpful suggestions I'd offered."

"You mean all the suggestions you made in your selfish, self-interested desire to coerce me into giving you a free ride back to Honolulu? Then, to top it off, you blackmailed me by taking advantage of my desperate circumstances."

"First, I didn't blackmail you into giving me a free ride," Bishop said, inserting the key card. "I offered to chip in for the fuel."

Bishop opened the door and nodded to Gabby to enter.

Gabby walked into the room, chose a bed, and flopped onto it.

"Well, I hope you're satisfied, Bishop. Because now I hate you even more than I already did."

"You don't hate me, Gabby. You're only angry with me."

Gabby sat up on the bed, her eyes blazing. "Don't you dare try to tell me how I feel."

"Fine. Can we just drop it? You said you didn't want me to say a word to you as a condition for accepting my generous offer to share the room. So, how about extending me the same courtesy?"

"Fine!" Gabby exclaimed.

Bishop checked the room and found his overnight bag was inside the closet. He carried it to the bed, opened it, and removed his shaving kit and clean underwear. He had been dreaming of a nice, hot shower for ages.

Gabby sprang off the bed. "I'm taking a shower," she announced before stomping into the bathroom and slamming the door.

"Petty," Bishop muttered, knowing she wanted to shower only because she realized he had intended to.

He went to the mini-refrigerator, opened it, and took out a bottle of Longboard Island Lager. After twisting off the cap, he sat down on his bed and drank some beer. A moment later, someone knocked on the door. He found a hotel staff member standing there with Gabby's suitcase when he opened the door. After taking the bag and thanking the employee, he closed the door. Then he tossed the suitcase on the bed Gabby had staked out without asking him which bed he wanted first. That seemed only common courtesy since it was his room, and she was the interloper.

Remembering he hadn't called Koko since arriving in Maui, Bishop took out his mobile and called her while he drank the beer. Koko answered on the second ring.

"Rick, where are you?" Koko exclaimed. "I've been worried sick since last night when you didn't come home!"

"I'm sorry, babe. Unfortunately, I'm in Maui. Things got complicated, and I didn't have a chance to call until now."

"What complications?"

"Well, I spent most of yesterday afternoon unconscious after someone hit me on the head with a pistol butt. Then I spent all day tracking down Alex Baker while fending off three guys trying to kill me."

"Oh my God, Rick. I hate your job. Can't you find something else to do?"

"Babe, you know it's the only thing I'm good at, and I'm finally growing my business."

"But we never see each other, Rick."

"We're just going through a rough patch, Koko. Soon, things will calm down and be smooth as glass. You'll see."

"So, are you coming home tonight?"

"No, I'm spending the night to get some rest, and I'll fly home in the morning."

"You promise you'll be back tomorrow?"

"Yes, sweetheart. I've done all I can here. So I need to get back to Honolulu to run down some leads there."

Rick heard Gabby shut off the water in the shower. He had to wrap up the call because he didn't want to risk Koko hearing Gabby's voice if she deigned to speak when she came out of the bathroom.

"Well, babe, I'm going to shower, grab some chow, and then catch some rack time. I'll come by the club to see you as soon as I get back to Honolulu tomorrow morning."

"Okay, Rick. I miss you, and I love you so much."

Love you back," Rick said. "Good night, and see you soon."

Bishop ended the call a second before Gabby opened the bathroom door and stepped out. Steam billowed from the bathroom into the room. Gabby wore a thick hotel terry-cloth robe and had wrapped her hair in a bath towel. She held her prostheses in her hand. The below the knee carbon fiber and titanium prosthetic limb was about ten inches long with an aviator's boot attached at the bottom. It was the one Gabby used for flying, but she had several variations with different shoe attachments. Gabby suffered the traumatic amputation of her left foot and part of her lower left leg during a tour as a Blackhawk helicopter pilot in Afghanistan.

Gabby hopped across the room on her right foot and sat down on the edge of her bed. Then she opened her suitcase, took out a prosthetic with a sneaker at the bottom, and put it on her stump. After selecting clean underwear from the suitcase, she stood up, turned her back to Bishop, and slipped them on beneath the robe. Sadly, the robe kept him from seeing anything interesting.

"I'm ordering a pizza from room service," Bishop said. "What do you want?"

"I'm not hungry."

"Come on, Gabby. Please. You have eaten nothing since breakfast, if then. I know you're hungry, and I'm buying."

"I said I'm not hungry!"

"Fine, but you're being so childish."

Bishop picked up the room phone receiver, called room service, and ordered a pizza and a bottle of red wine. Then he grabbed his shaving kit and clean underwear and went into the bathroom. After showering, shaving, and brushing his teeth, he put on the other robe over his boxers. When he exited the bathroom, he saw Gabby hadn't dressed either, although she had removed the towel from her head.

He grabbed another beer but didn't offer Gabby anything from the minibar since it seemed obvious she didn't intend to behave civilly. A few minutes later, room service delivered the pizza and wine with two plates, glasses, and silverware.

Bishop carried the pizza to the small table, sat down, and opened the wine. After filling his glass, he opened the pizza box and started eating.

When Bishop started on his second slice, Gabby got off the bed and sat down on the other chair at the table. I'll have a slice if there is enough.

"Help yourself," Bishop said, sliding the second plate over. "There's plenty. If there isn't, I'll order more." Then he uncorked the wine bottle and filled the other glass for Gabby.

Gabby ate silently for a few minutes. Then she said, "Did you order this kind because you know it's my favorite? Is this a peace offering?"

Bishop considered lying, but didn't. "I ordered it because I like Canadian bacon and pineapple pizza. But I'm happy you like it too."

"Uh-huh. I should have known. You only ever think of yourself."

She took a second slice.

"Whatever, Gabby."

"Well, it's true, isn't it?"

"No."

"Then why have you never even apologized for what you did, Rick?"

"I apologized. I emailed you. And I'm sure Koko told you I had to fly directly to Los Angeles for another case as soon as I finished the one on the Big Island."

"You think an email sufficed? You could have called. And you've had opportunities to come to me with a face-to-face apology since you got back. But you didn't bother."

Rick said nothing, which seemed only to make Gabby angrier.

"And the email was total bullshit. You dumped me because you knew I deserved someone better? What a load of crap."

"Technically, I didn't dump you. We were never together, Gabby."

"Oh, right. You only rejected me," Gabby said, pouring herself more wine. "You spent months trying to get into my pants. Then when you wore me down, and I wanted to have sex, suddenly you weren't interested."

"I made a mistake, Gabby, and I'm sorry. I never intended to hurt you. Our friendship is something I miss. And I am very fond of you, whether you believe that or not."

"It was only ever a stupid game for you, Rick. I know that now. You never wanted me. I was so stupid."

"That's not true, Gabby."

"Was it my leg? Was that the huge turnoff for you? Is that why you didn't want me that day in Hawaii?"

"I can't believe you even asked that," Bishop said, growing annoyed. "You know that makes no difference, Gabby. It's one of the many things I admire about you. You never complain. You don't behave like you have any disability, but just carry on like any non-disabled person and get on with your life. And you are an attractive, desirable woman."

"Then why didn't you want me?"

"I wanted you," Bishop said. "More than you know."

"But you want Koko more?"

"It isn't about that, Gabby. I was with Koko first, before I met you. But I wanted you in the worst way. I just realized I was being selfish, and if I started something with you, it wouldn't have been fair to you or Koko. So I only tried to do the right thing."

Gabby emptied the rest of the wine into her glass and sat silently sipping it.

"I truly am sorry, Gabby," Bishop said. "I should never have come on to you, and I'm sorry I ruined our friendship. It meant a lot to me. And you do too."

Gabby finished the wine and stood up. "If you've finished eating, can you turn off the lights so I can undress and get into bed?"

"Sure," Bishop said. He tossed the empty box and bottle in the trash can and then walked over and flipped the light switch. Then, feeling his way to his bed, he turned down the covers, took off the bathrobe, and got beneath the sheets.

In the dim outside light coming through the window, he watched Gabby sitting on the bed, removing her prosthetic limb. Then she shrugged out of the bathrobe. Feeling the all too familiar ache, Bishop turned over on his side to face the wall.

"What hurt most was you weren't fair to us, Rick," Gabby said.

"How do you mean I wasn't fair?"

"We've never made love, but Koko lives with you, and I'm sure you make love to her all the time. You don't even know what it might be like with us. I would have accepted it if you had made love to me in that motel room that day and then decided you wanted to stay with Koko. At least it would have been fair. At least I would have believed you gave us a chance."

"Gabby, I thought it would only make things worse and would only hurt you and Koko. That's why I couldn't go through with it. But I wanted to. You were so beautiful. I wanted you more than anything."

"You mean that, Rick? You truly wanted me?"

"Yes. I hate myself for it, but I've never stopped."

Gabby said nothing, but Bishop thought she was crying softly. He felt like a first-class jerk.

After several minutes, he felt the covers lifting and then Gabby sliding into bed beside him. He felt her pressing her bare skin against his.

"If we made love just once, I could feel you've been fair to us, Rick. I could believe you truly desired me. And I swear it. I'd accept it if you felt you still wanted to stay with Koko afterward. And I could trust you again, and we could fix our broken friendship."

Bishop groaned quietly. Then he felt Gabby's hand gently stroking his body.

"Gabby, we shouldn't."

"Please, Rick. Am I asking for so much?"

Bishop knew he should say no and accept it if Gabby said she hated him. But he couldn't.

CHAPTER SIXTEEN

Two Can Play That Game

BISHOP WOKE UP FEELING guilty, confused, and anguishing over what he'd done. Sleeping with Gabby was far different from sleeping with Gemma Nelson in Hawaii that time after Koko had broken up with him for a day. That hadn't been cheating, technically. He'd been temporarily single. This time, he'd been unfaithful and couldn't deny it. Why hadn't he paid for separate rooms instead of coercing Gabby to stay in his room to guilt her into giving him and Greenwood a ride back to Honolulu? Now he had probably screwed everything up. How could he live with himself? Then he felt Gabby's fingertips stroking his chest and then his stomach. He looked over at her. Her head on her hand, propped with an elbow. Gabby looked at him, smiling. Her eyes twinkled. The fingertips marched downward.

"Gabby? No. Last night you said one time."

"Um, that was last night, Rick. Before I knew it was even better than I'd ever dreamed it would be with you. Oh my God, Rick. You were such an animal. And we already have to shower, anyway."

"Gabby, we can't."

"Why not? Face it, Rick. You cheated on Koko, and I've already betrayed my best friend by sleeping with her man. The genie is out of the bottle, and we can't put it back. Does twice change things any when we've already done it once?"

"It isn't right, Gabby."

Bishop jerked when Gabby squeezed. She grinned. "Obviously, you want to, so why don't you stop fighting it, tiger?"

An hour later, Bishop carried Gabby into the bathroom in his arms. After showering together, he carried her back into the room, and they got dressed. Then they packed their bags and took the elevator down to the lobby. Gabby put her arms around his neck and kissed him passionately.

They saw Greenwood sitting in the lobby and walked over when they exited the elevator.

"Good morning," Greenwood said.

"Good morning, Lynch," Gabby said. "Sleep well?"

"Yes, I did, thanks. But I'm an early riser."

"You want to get breakfast?" Bishop said.

"Oh no, but you two go ahead," Greenwood said. "I'll wait here."

Bishop turned to Gabby. "Hey, can you grab us a table in the restaurant? I need to ask Lynch something, and then I'll meet you inside."

"Sure, sweetie," Gabby said with a smile. "See you in a few." Then she turned and walked toward the restaurant entrance.

"Well, did someone kiss and make up?" Greenwood chuckled. "I assume you scored us that ride back to Honolulu. Pun intended."

"Yeah, I did," Bishop said, his face flushing. "But I had to sell my soul to do it."

"Well, thanks for taking one for the team, man."

What do you mean?"

"It's obvious," Greenwood said. "I know the post-coital blissful look when I see it. She's a happy woman. And you've got lipstick on your cheek."

Bishop hastily wiped his cheek with his hand.

"Hey," he said. "I know you said you're a little short. But come and have breakfast with us, my treat. Then we'll head to the airport."

"You sure?" Greenwood said. "I don't want to be a charity case, and you've already offered to help me out when we get to Honolulu."

"Don't worry about it, Brian. Now come on. I'm starving."

"Well, if you insist."

***

Bishop and Greenwood stood on the tarmac watching as Gabby did her pre-flight checks after arranging for a tanker to fuel her bird.

"So, you said you have a girlfriend living with you," Greenwood said. "But I don't blame you. Gabby is a gorgeous woman. I sure couldn't turn down a woman like that if I had the chance. Girlfriend at home or not."

"Well, it wasn't like I planned it. It just happened."

"I'm in awe, bud. After the way she treated you yesterday, you must really have a way with the ladies, Bishop. I didn't believe you could even talk her into giving us a ride."

Bishop explained the circumstances about how Abigail Stone had canceled their rooms and how Gabby hadn't expected to pay for her room because Stone was supposed to pay. So she hadn't brought money or credit cards. Then he told Greenwood he had used Gabby's financial circumstances as leverage to guilt her into giving them the ride. He'd coerced her into staying in his room so she would feel like she owed it to him to give them a lift back to Honolulu.

"It was a dumb idea," Bishop said. "I should have paid for her room. But I never dreamed we'd end up in bed together as angry as she was with me."

"And now you feel guilty as hell for cheating on your girlfriend? I get it, dude. I'd feel guilty too if I cheated on someone I was in a relationship with."

"Thanks for that, Brian. I feel so much better now."

"Don't get me wrong, bud. I'm not judging you. I'm just saying."

"Now, I don't know what to do," Bishop said.

"Well, a word to the wise," Greenwood said. "Don't let the guilt make you believe you should confess to your girlfriend. I had a buddy once who did that. That made things even worse. Believe me, even if a woman thinks you're cheating, they don't want to know for sure. So you better just keep your mouth shut and learn to live with it."

Gabby had the rotors turning and waved them to get aboard. She insisted Bishop ride in the front this time, so Greenwood got in the back. On the flight back, Gabby reached over and stroked Bishop's thigh from time to time. Bishop had a sense of foreboding that things would only worsen after his unwise decision.

After landing in Honolulu, Gabby asked Bishop for a word before he and Greenwood left. Greenwood walked away to give them some privacy.

"I just wanted to thank you for making things better, Rick," Gabby said. "I've missed our friendship, too. And I'll keep my promise. I won't pressure you to leave Koko."

"I appreciate that, Gabby. I feared I'd only made things worse, but being with you meant so much to me. So I'm glad you feel better about things, and I'm so glad we're still friends. But I'm a little confused now, and I can't make any promises."

"I understand," Gabby said, beaming. Then she patted Bishop's face gently. "*Rawr*, tiger."

Bishop chuckled. "Well, I'll see you, and thanks again for the ride."

"No problem," Gabby said.

Bishop nodded and turned to walk away.

"Hey, Rick, one more thing."

Bishop turned back and smiled. Gabby walked to him and then leaned in to whisper in his ear.

"Rick, darling, you blackmailed me into giving you the ride back. And two can play that game. I meant what I said about not pressuring you to leave Koko. But remember this. Whenever I make a booty call, you better come running.

Otherwise, I'm going to tell Koko everything with very graphically detailed descriptions."

Then Gabby kissed him on the cheek and turned and walked toward her office.

Bishop felt a sinking feeling in the pit of his stomach. Yes, he'd made things worse. Much worse.

CHAPTER SEVENTEEN

Facing the Music

KOKO MAHELONA HAD HIGH cheekbones and warm brown skin and a mass of dark brown hair that reached the middle of her back. She rarely wore makeup because she didn't need it. Unlike most of the women Bishop had been with, even after all the time they had been together, looking at Koko still took his breath away. Well, usually, but not today. Instead of the big warm brown eyes that always did sparkly things when Koko was happy, today the same eyes were flashing a storm warning.

Koko Mahelona clearly wasn't happy and Rick Bishop was the reason. When he'd walked into the bar, Joe Rose glanced up but then quickly buried his face in his newspaper as if he'd suddenly discovered an absorbing news article. Koko had skewered Bishop with an ireful stare the moment he walked through the door. To add insult to injury, Koko hadn't even grabbed and opened a Longboard Island Lager to set on the bar in front of him, when Bishop sat down at the bar on a stool. She stood with her arms crossed and her butt leaning against the beer cooler behind her.

"What's wrong, babe?" Bishop asked tentatively, feeling even more guilty about what he'd done in Maui now that he was face to face with Koko.

Koko's eyes flashed and then narrowed almost at once.

"I beg your pardon?" she said. "What do you think is wrong, Richard?"

"I don't know, Koko," Bishop said, holding up his open hands in a gesture of helplessness. "I called, and I told you I'd come by as soon as I got back to Honolulu. And here I am."

"I've talked with Gabby," Koko spat before her lips compressed into a hard, thin line.

Bishop gulped involuntarily and felt a sudden burning sensation in the pit of his stomach.

"Wait, I can explain—"

"Gabby told me she flew you back from Maui and got back almost three hours ago," Koko interrupted. "That doesn't sound like you came right over as soon as you got back. Where have you been?"

Bishop almost swooned in relief. If that's all Gabby had told her, he might survive this inquisition.

"Well, did she mention she had another passenger besides me?" Bishop said. "I ran into an old buddy in Maui from the Navy, Brian Greenwood. He's had a financial setback, so I offered to help him out with a place to stay for a few days until he gets back on his feet."

Koko's mouth dropped open, and she looked as if her head might explode. "Richard Bishop, if you've invited a friend to stay over at the apartment, I sure hope you enjoy each other's company, because I'll be moving back in with mom."

Bishop chuckled. "I'm not an idiot, Koko. We don't have room for a guest at the apartment, even for only a few days. I'm letting Brian bunk at my office. So, when we got back, we had to stop at the store and my storage unit to pick up some basics, and then I had to take him to the office and get him settled in. Then I came straight here."

Behind his newspaper, Joe Rose stifled a laugh.

"You're letting some guy live in your office?" Koko asked incredulously. "Do you actually think Mrs. Wong will be okay with that arrangement?"

"Brian will be gone long before that old battle axe finds out," Bishop said good naturedly. "And I've already warned Brian about her, so he'll keep a low profile."

Koko shook her head and then raised her eyes to the ceiling. Finally, she eyed Bishop again after what Bishop assumed was her habit of taking deep breaths and counting to ten when he said something she found annoying.

"Okay," she said. "Do you think you might drop by the apartment tonight for a change?"

"Of course, I'll be home tonight," Bishop said. "Why wouldn't I be?"

"Oh, I don't know. Maybe because you didn't come home two nights ago without even bothering to call. Then you spent another night in Maui last night before bothering to come back here. Now you've got this new buddy I've never heard of living in your office. I thought maybe you would be way too busy to show up at the apartment."

"Koko, be reasonable," Rick protested. "I explained all that when I called you last evening."

"Hm, oh yes, when you called after not coming home the night before and then sounded like you couldn't wait to get off the phone with me?"

"Babe, I was worn out and my head was still killing me after that guy pistol whipped me."

"You better be at the apartment when I get home, Richard Bishop," Koko said firmly. "And you better have a nice dinner prepared, and I'm not talking about Spam sandwiches and macaroni salad. Feel me?"

"Yes, Koko, and I'm sorry you're so upset. I swear I'll make it all up to you."

"Richard, after dinner, you and I are going to have a serious talk. I'm sick of you being out late or out of town all the time. It's taking a toll on our relationship and I won't put up with things the way they are much longer. I'm just giving you fair warning."

"Understood," Bishop said meekly. "I only wanted to make my business successful for us, babe. That's why I've been working so much. But I'm prepared to make whatever adjustments it takes to keep things great with us."

"You better be," Koko said. Then she turned and went into the back room.

"Damn, Richard," Joe said, finally putting his paper down. "You're walking on the jagged edge with Koko and you better up your game, pal."

"Joe, you're a business owner like me. You know it takes hard work and long hours to make a business successful."

"Richard, a man's business is his business, but I've known you for a long time. And my guess is there is something else going on with you besides a sudden interest in becoming a business success. You pulled your weight when we were in the teams together. But let's face it, pal. As a civilian, you're the laziest guy I know."

"That was low, Joe," Bishop said. "You really hit me below the belt with that one."

Rose laughed. "Richard, you were lucky to work a four-hour day when you bothered to work at all. You sat in your office and waited for walk-ins instead of getting out and beating the bushes for clients. I just have a hard time believing you've suddenly got so busy you have to work twelve-hour days and go out of town all the time. You want to tell me her name?"

"I'm hurt you would even say such a thing in jest, Joe. You know how committed I am to Koko."

Rose rolled his eyes. "And who is this Brian Greenwood character? I don't remember anyone by that name from the Navy."

"Well, Brian was in the Navy, but actually, I only met him a couple of days ago. And he is going through a rough patch financially and I am helping him out. Speaking of that, he needs a job. Is there any way you could put him on the payroll here?"

"What qualifications does he have? Bartending, food prep?"

"Well, we haven't discussed it, but I'm sure he has skills you could use."

"One of my cooks is going on vacation. I guess, assuming he can cook, I could take him on a trial basis to fill in. Then, depending on how it works out, maybe

I could keep him on afterwards. Why don't you bring him by and I'll talk to him?"

"Sounds perfect," Bishop said. "I'm sure he's qualified to do something in the kitchen. Preparing bar food isn't rocket science, exactly."

"What did he do in the Navy?"

"Supply and logistics. He got out as an E-6 and held a pretty important billet in Afghanistan." Bishop saw no reason to get into how NCIS had arrested Brian for malfeasance and that he had spent five years in Leavenworth before getting dishonorably discharged.

"Okay, bring him around tomorrow morning and we'll talk," Rose said.

"Is Koko busy in the back, or is she just mad at me?" Rick asked.

"Both," Joe said. "But she is working on the inventory so she can get out the orders to our suppliers at the end of the week."

"Okay," Bishop said. "I'm going to get out of here. I'll see her at home later, and I need to figure out something for dinner."

"A word to the wise, Richard. Better make it good."

Bishop nodded, then he said goodbye to Rose and left the bar.

CHAPTER EIGHTEEN

Remember Pearl Harbor

IT WAS ABOUT HALF past ten in the morning when Bishop arrived at his office on Hotel Street. After parking the Toyota in his designated spot in the alley behind his building next to the smelly dumpster, Bishop made his way around to the front. There he paused and quick peeked around the corner of the building. The coast was clear, with no sign of Mrs. Wong. Since the woman's Chinese herbal shop did little business, Mrs. Wong spent most of her time out front sweeping the sidewalk endlessly with her fan broom. Bishop assumed she was inside drinking tea and watching the weed smoking, commie morons on MSLSD celebrating the latest revelations leaked by the January 6th Select Committee that was holding their Stalinist-like purge hearings over the so-called capital insurrection.

Like most Americans, Bishop hadn't followed the hearings and knew little about the fake insurrection other than the media propagandists considered it the worst thing that had happened to the country since the Teapot Dome scandal. Bishop sprinted to the glass door leading to the stairs to his second-floor walk-up and slipped inside. The last thing he needed after the soul-crushing discussion with Koko the previous evening was an encounter with Mrs. Wong.

Koko had issued an ultimatum. She expected Rick to be at home every evening when she arrived from work, to limit his out-of-town investigations to the bare minimum, and to show her the attention and devotion she deserved. Otherwise, Koko vowed she'd move out of the apartment and back into her old room at her mother's house.

Bishop had meekly agreed to all his girlfriend's demands, mostly because he felt guilty about diddling her best friend Gabby a couple of times back in that Maui hotel room. But given the pressure Gabby had now brought to bear by blackmailing him, Bishop wondered if it might not be better if Koko moved out for a while. That would give him some breathing space while he developed a plan to escape Gabby's clutches. Why did women have to be so difficult? He unlocked his office door and went inside.

What he saw shocked Bishop when he walked in. Greenwood had swept and mopped the entire place and had even dusted the blades of the old ceiling fan. His new temporary sub-tenant had already folded and neatly put away the army cot and sleeping bag Bishop had pulled out of his storage unit and loaned him. Greenwood glanced up from where he sat behind the worn desk, looking at Bishop's old laptop screen. Rick walked to the desk and plunked down the greasy Mickey D's bag he'd carried inside.

"I stopped on the way in and grabbed you a couple of McMuffins for breakfast, buddy," Bishop said.

"Hey, thanks," Greenwood said, reaching into the bag. "I cleaned up the place a little," Greenwood said while chewing a mouthful of eggs, cheese, savory sausage, and toasted English muffin.

"Yeah, the place looks swell," Bishop said, walking to the table holding his single serve coffee brewer. He put a cup beneath the dispenser, selected one of the cheap generic coffee pods from the cardboard box next to the coffee maker, and popped it inside before hitting the brew button.

"You know," said Greenwood, "if you bought some paint, I could repaint the walls. Lord knows this dive could use a little sprucing up."

"It's something to think about," Bishop said, sipping his freshly brewed coffee. "But I arranged a job interview for you, so you may be too busy working to do any painting."

"Seriously? You already found me a job?"

"Pretty much. You have to go for an interview, but that's mostly only a formality."

"What's the job?"

Bishop told Greenwood all about his discussion the previous afternoon with his best bud, Joe Rose.

"You have any food prep skills?" Bishop asked.

"Yeah," Greenwood said. "I worked at an In-N-Out burger joint when I was in high school and I was the best fry guy they had. And I also worked in the kitchen at Leavenworth. So, I'm good to go for kitchen work. Also, I spent plenty of time in dive bars when I was in the Navy, so I could tend bar too if your bud needs help with that."

"Well, Joe is looking to hire you to cover for one of his cooks who is going on vacation," Bishop said. "But I'm sure the sky is the limit at Joe's club and you can work your way up the ladder."

"When is the interview?"

"The sooner the better. I've got to run out to Pearl this morning, so I'll drop you off at the Likelike Club for your interview on the way."

Bishop dug into his pocket and handed Greenwood a handful of change. "That's for bus fare back here in case Joe doesn't need you to work today," he said.

"Thanks, man," Greenwood said, pocketing the change. "I really appreciate you helping me out, dude."

"No problem, bro," Bishop said. "But a word to the wise. I wouldn't mention anything to Joe about your stretch at Leavenworth. Joe's a law-and-order man all the way. I think your In-N-Out Burger bona fides establish your food prep skills well enough."

"Okay," Greenwood said, swallowing the last of the second McMuffin. Then he wadded the bag and tossed it at the trash can, which was already running over.

"Well, let's get going," Bishop said. "Since you cleaned everything else, you might as well grab that bag of trash and bring it along. I'm parked in back beside the dumpster so it's on the way."

Greenwood nodded, and grabbed the filled liner from the trash can, packed it down, and tied the top in a knot. Then they left the office. After Rick locked up and they took the stairs down to the first floor, Bishop stopped before pushing out through the glass door.

"Better let me hold the trash bag in case we run into my Chicom landlady," he said. "That way, if she questions me about you, as she might since she sticks her nose into all my business, I'll tell her you're a client."

Greenwood nodded and handed over the plastic bag. Then they went out the door. Sure enough, Mrs. Wong was in front of the building, sweeping the sidewalk.

"Good morning, Mrs. Wong," Bishop said pleasantly. "Beautiful morning, isn't it?"

The old women glared at Bishop, wrinkling her nose as she raised and tightened her upper lip into a scornful frown.

"Mr. Rick, you no clean oil spill from your car in the alley. If city fine me, Mr. Rick, you will pay. Understand?"

"Sorry, Mrs. Wong," Bishop said contritely. "I have to run out to Pearl, but I'll get right on that oil spill when I get back."

"You better," said Wong, casting a suspicious glance at Greenwood. "Who this man? One of your worthless friends?"

"No, Mrs. Wong," Bishop said. "This is Dominic Waters, a client. We were discussing a problem he needs my help with up in my office."

"Hello, Mrs. Wong," Greenwood said, extending his hand. "Good to meet you." Ignoring him, Wong turned away and went back to sweeping.

"Come on, Dominic," Bishop said. "I'll be happy to drop you at your place of business on my way out to Pearl."

The two men hurried around the corner of the building to the alley. Bishop tossed the trash bag onto the overflowing dumpster and they got into his Toyota. When he turned the key, the ancient Corolla roared to life, backfired, and belched blue smoke. Once the clanking sound of the engine leveled out, or came as close to it as it ever did, Rick reversed and drove down the alley. He made a right from the alley and a left onto Hotel Street at the intersection.

"I thought that you private eyes all drove flash cars," Greenwood shouted over the engine noise.

"This is the real world Brian," Bishop said, fighting the wheel to keep the car in a single lane of traffic. He figured the powering steering pump reservoir was low on fluid again. "Not *Grand Theft Auto.*"

"Huh? I don't remember there being any private eyes in that video game and I've played it a lot."

"No, Brian, there are no private investigator characters in the game," Bishop scoffed. "But there are lots of flashy cars. I thought that was what we were discussing. Cars."

"Oh. Right, bro. I got you, man."

Ten minutes later, Bishop rolled up in front of the Likelike Club and the Toyota squeaked to a stop.

"Joe is an awesome dude," he said. "Just keep Leavenworth and your DD out of the discussion, and you are sure to get the job."

"Got it," Brian said, yanking on his door handle.

"Hang on," Bishop said. "The handle doesn't work. I've been intending to get my mechanic to have a look at it." Getting out, he hot-footed it around the front of the car and opened the door for Greenwood.

"Thanks for the ride," Greenwood said. "Guess I'll catch you later back at the office."

Bishop nodded, wished Greenwood good luck with his interview, and got back behind the wheel of the Toyota. As Greenwood walked through the door into the club, Rick mashed the accelerator and the car rumbled down the street.

A half hour after dropping Greenwood off, Rick rolled up to the gate at Pearl Harbor, the iconic naval base the Japanese had attacked in 1941, the Corolla's engine ticking like a cheap watch. The Marine sentry at the gate eyed the car with suspicion as it belched clouds of thick, blue smoke from the exhaust pipe. He figured the vehicle was a rolling EPA violation. Bishop held up his Naval Reserves ID card and the lance corporal inspected it.

"Where are you going on the base, sir?" the Marine asked, fanning the stinky, oily smoke away from his face, which was searing his nasal passages.

"I'm here to see NCIS Special Agent Bob Utley." Bishop said.

"Roger, sir," the guard said, penciling Bishop's information on the form attached to his clipboard. He wondered whether he should phone the Sergeant of the Guard to see if he had the authority to arrest for multiple plain view EPA violations. No wonder Buddha Jeg, the Buddhist holy man the dementia plagued non-birthing individual occupying the White House had appointed as Secretary of Transportation was so adamant about forcing Americans to buy electric cars. The change couldn't come soon enough for Lance Corporal Hinkley. Deciding against calling the SOG because it might require paperwork, Hinkley handed Bishop a pass and then waved him through the gate. Rick snapped a quick salute to the USMC dog-faced pony soldier and gunned the engine. The Toyota's engine wheezed and then the transmission engaged and the Corolla thundered through the gate onto the base.

As Bishop drove along, he looked at the buildings he passed with dismay, wondering how the Navy had learned nothing since the Japanese zeros had appeared over Diamond Head and dive-bombed and torpedoed the base eighty some years before. He figured the Navy should get busy camouflaging the buildings since Nancy Peloton, or whatever the hell the vodka swilling drunk's name was, the current Speaker of the House of Non-Representatives, had pissed off the CCP government in Beijing by visiting Taiwan. Bishop feared any day now, the Chicoms would stage Pearl Harbor part deux in retaliation for her treating them like a bunch of drag queens at the Republican National Convention.

Rick drove up to the building housing NCIS headquarters and shut off the engine. Getting out, he strode up the steps to the front doors as the Corolla continued to shudder and the engine knocked loudly behind him. At the receptionist desk, he gave his name and asked to see Special Agent Utley. The receptionist buzzed Utley's office. A few minutes later the agent entered the lobby from a corridor.

"Rick Bishop, it's been a minute bud," Utley said, taking Bishop's hand and pumping it enthusiastically. "It's damn good to see you again, brother."

Bishop had served with Utley when they were both in the SEALS before Utley left the teams to take a civilian position with NCIS.

"If you can spare me five minutes, I'd like to pick your brain about something," Rick said.

"Sure, not a problem," Utley said. "Come on back to my office."

Bishop followed Utley to his office and sat down in a visitor's chair while Utley settled himself behind his desk.

"I hope I'm not interrupting something important," he said as Utley reached over to shut down his desktop computer.

"Not at all," Utley said. "I was just finishing up the mandatory CRT online training module I've been avoiding."

"That sucks," Bishop said. "I'm glad I got out of the Navy before the woke jihadis took over the Pentagon."

"I hear you," Utley said. "I never heard of white privilege until this crap started up. It's unreal. But if you don't complete the training, you might as well walk around with a white hood over your head. So, what did you want to know?"

On a hunch, Bishop asked, "You ever know an NCIS agent by the name of Craig Lynch?"

"Hell yes," Utley said with a grin. "We worked together at Navy Yard in DC before I transferred out here to Pearl."

Bishop felt a jolt of excitement. "Do you know if Lynch worked any cases in the Stan? Like a case where four DOD contractors stole $10 million from a Navy finance facility in Kabul?"

Utley's eyes widened in surprise. "How do you know about that?"

"I'll explain everything in a moment, bro. Just humor me and tell me whatever you can."

"Okay," Utley said, bending forward over the desk and lowering his voice. "I shouldn't talk about it, but we go way back and I know I can trust you. That was an FBI case, but Craig went to Kabul as the Navy liaison on the task force investigating the theft. The money had been in a Navy facility like you said, but belonged to the State Department and was earmarked for a congressional initiated gender studies program and for bribes to key Afghan government officials, State was paying off to grease the skids to put the program in place. But they didn't identify the suspects until Craig arrested a Navy supply guy on an unrelated charge. He knew who the heist suspects were and gave up their names as part of a plea deal on his charges."

"That's what I've heard," Bishop said. "One last question, and then I'll read you into my interest in it all. Do you know if Lynch lost his badge and credentials while he was in Kabul?"

"Yes, he did," Utley said, even more astonished. "Craig told me he went to interview the supply guy at the brig and had his credentials when he arrived there. But later, back at his hotel, he found his wallet missing from his pocket."

Mystery solved. Bishop had discovered where Brian Greenwood had got his phony NCIS credentials. And they hadn't been phony at all, just stolen legit credentials.

"I've got my own private investigations shop," Bishop said. "I took a case recently and got sucked into that heist case. And I know who has the money and even encountered all four of the guys who stole it."

"Here is Hawaii? The FBI had a line on them briefly in Long Beach, but lost them and they have been in the wind ever since."

"As recently as a day ago, they were in Maui," Bishop said. "But I'm pretty sure the cash is here in Honolulu or on Oahu somewhere, at least."

"Damn, bro. I'd love busting those guys. Breaking that case would be a career maker for me with the agency. Do you know where they are now?"

"No," Bishop admitted. "I last saw them in Maui, but I figure the cash is here and eventually they will all be back in Honolulu."

Utley leaned back in his chair, smiling. "I know you well, bro, so what's your angle? I know you aren't working for the government on this."

Bishop grinned. "No, I'm not selflessly running around trying to recover the government's money for them," he admitted. "I heard the Treasury gives rewards to those who help recover stolen government money. And I'm angling to collect the reward if I can find the $10 million."

"That's true," Utley said. "Ten to thirty percent, depending on the amount. I'd say $10 million falls into the twenty percent range easily."

Bishop nodded enthusiastically. "Okay, here is what I propose," he said. "I'll keep searching for the money, and meanwhile, if I have any further contact with those four guys, I'll call you and tell you how to find them. You can make the bust, and if I find the cash, I'll turn it over to you and you will be my government rep to confirm to the Treasury I recovered it. The government gets their $10 million back less what they pay me as a reward."

"You really think you can find it?"

"That's what I do, bro," Bishop said. "Finding people and finding stuff is my business. And I know the guy well who has the money or at least knows where it is. I know how he thinks, so I'm confident I'll figure it out."

"Okay, Rick," Utley said. "You've never steered me wrong. You've got a deal, brother."

CHAPTER NINETEEN

Meanwhile

Daniel K. Inouye International Airport, Honolulu

MARK PRESTON COVERED HIS mouth and yawned before pulling his ringing phone out of his pocket and answering it.

"What have you got, Smitty?" he said into the phone.

"Still no sign of Baker or the woman," the caller said. "You want us to stay here and keep watching the airport?"

"Did you talk to the chick you met who works for the airline?"

"Yeah, she says their names haven't shown up on any manifests for departures and they haven't booked a flight out."

"Well, I guess that means they are still in Maui somewhere," Preston said. "And that says they aren't planning to fly back to the mainland from there, as Baker led us to believe. Now I think that was only a diversion."

"So, what do we do?"

"You and Jason catch a flight back here to Honolulu," Preston said. "I can't continue sitting on Honolulu International alone. I can barely keep my eyes open. They will eventually try to get a flight out, but now I feel sure the money is here in Honolulu. Our best option is to wait them out here."

"Okay, but we're running low on cash and all our credit cards are almost maxed out. We have to find Baker fast."

"Yeah, tell me about it. Just get back here as soon as you can."

"Okay," the caller said, and then he disconnected.

Preston put his phone away. No way he was leaving Hawaii without the $10 million, or whatever was left of it. When Smitty and Jason arrived, they would pull a robbery if necessary to get the cash to stay on the hunt. But they had to keep a low profile. Since that PI had gotten away, he may have gone to the feds and the FBI might already be looking for them. Surely Baker knew that too, so Preston figured he'd come back to Honolulu to get the money sooner rather than later. All they had to do was nab him when he did.

Hāna Bay Beach Park, Hāna, Maui

Sitting on mats on the sand at Hāna Bay Beach Park, Alex Baker rubbed sun tan lotion on Abby Stone's shapely, muscular shoulders and back. After escaping from Preston and the boys and Rick Bishop, they had made the four-hour drive along the northeast coast of Maui on Hawaii Route 36 to Hāna. There they rented under assumed names a room at the E Komo Mai Inn, a small bed and breakfast near the beach park, and had paid cash. Baker felt certain Preston wouldn't find them there, and he doubted Bishop was looking for them at all. He had hated double-crossing his old bud from the teams, but Baker hadn't liked the way he'd seen Stone looking at Bishop. Now that he was close to getting away with the money for good, he wanted to hang on to Stone, the most passionate woman he'd ever been with. And knowing how much Abby loved the finer things, Baker figured ten million bucks would hold her interest. Especially since he had no intention of splitting the money with her as he'd promised. If he did that, she'd take the money and run off somewhere alone.

"Since we haven't gone to Kahului Airport to board a flight to some country that doesn't extradite to the U.S., I suppose you stashed the money back in Honolulu," Stone purred as Baker worked the lotion into her soft skin.

"Indeed," Baker said as he continued working his way down her back toward her gorgeous bikini-clad bottom. "I only used Maui as a diversion. Preston and the boys can't have the unlimited capital to finance a long-term stay in Hawaii. I expect they will give up and head back to the mainland soon, if they didn't buy my story and have left already."

"Somehow, I don't feel he bought the story that we intended to fly directly to the mainland," Stone said. "So, what is your plan now?"

"We'll give it another day and then we'll go back to Honolulu, pick up the money, and fly out from Honolulu International."

"Well, since they probably believe you have the money with you, don't you think they are watching the airport here? We're bound to run into them trying to get a flight back to Honolulu?"

"I've considered that. That's why we will not catch a commercial flight back. Instead, I'll hire a helicopter service at Hāna Airport to fly us back."

"I still think we should have had that female pilot I hired in the first place fly us back to Honolulu yesterday. I'd already paid for the round trip."

"I didn't trust her after I found out she knew Bishop," Baker said. "And Rick was a wildcard. I wasn't sure what he might do. Besides, I wanted some alone time with you here on Maui, and we've had good times, haven't we?"

"Mm, yes have," Stone said, turning to kiss Baker on the lips. "And I'm about ready to go back to room and have more good times."

Baker laughed. "You could talk me into that."

"Don't you think you should tell me where the money is?" Stone said. "You know, just in case. If they grabbed you, I could still get away with it and wait for you to join me."

Baker grinned. "Oh no, mon amor. What kind of man would subject the woman he loves to such temptation?"

Pouting, Stone stuck out her bottom lip. "After all that we've been through together, you still don't trust me?"

"I trust you implicitly, darling," Baker said with a grin. "As long as I'm the only one who knows where the ten million is. But don't worry, once we're safely away from Hawaii, you will get your share. I promise."

"Okay," Stone said, standing and bending to pick up her mat with her exquisite bikini-clad bottom inches from Baker's face. "Then let's go back to the room and think about something other than the money for a while. Shall we?"

"Indeed," Baker said, jumping to his feet. "Lead on, darling girl."

Pearl City, Hawaii

Rick was in high spirits as he drove away from the navy base, even though the Corolla's engine temperature was climbing ominously. If he could find that money, Utley had as good as told him he'd get a two-million-dollar reward. That meant he'd soon be trading up from this beast to a flashy, foreign sports car instead of settling for only a Mustang or Camaro on payments. And he'd have enough cash to leave Hawaii with Koko for a while until things with Gabby settled down. He'd only have to get a hold of Koko's phone long enough to delete Gabby's number after blocking her calls to Koko's phone. Sure, he admitted that making whoopee with Gabby had been amazing. The woman seemed insatiable. But he couldn't keep that up. Not that he didn't already feel guilty for cheating on Koko, but if he continued sleeping with Gabby as she demanded, he knew somehow Koko would find out and then she'd kill him.

Bishop's phone dinged with an incoming text. Fishing the phone out of his jacket pocket, he gaped at the screen with horror. Then he cursed and slammed a fist on the steering wheel when he read Gabby's text.

Booty call baby. Better come running. My place in half an hour.

Bishop had expected he still had a day or two to figure a way out of the Gabby man trap. But she already wanted him now. Looking at the time on the phone screen, he felt grateful that at least Koko was at work and wouldn't get off for another six hours. He had time to satisfy Gabby and still get home in time to shower and fix something for dinner before Koko got there. So Bishop pointed the Corolla toward Gabby's duplex on Pacific Heights Road. He might as well get it over with.

Twenty-eight minutes later, with two minutes to spare, he parked the Corolla in the driveway.

Gabby rented a small two-bedroom frame house in the Nuuanu-Punchbowl neighborhood. When he rang the bell, Gabby opened the door wearing only a smile with a floral-lace cropped bustier and matching panties. She grabbed Bishop's tie and yanked him through the open doorway. Then after closing the door, she shoved his back against it and greedily sought his lips with hers while her hands groped and squeezed his butt through his slacks. Then, again grabbing his tie, she led Bishop to her boudoir.

Once in the bedroom, she continued kissing him ardently while she efficiently stripped off his jacket, shirt, and slacks before putting a hand on his chest and shoving him backwards onto the king-sized bed. After yanking his boxers off, she climbed atop him and ground her scantily clad body against him as she continued kissing him hard on the mouth. Afterward, once she had Bishop in the condition she wanted, she rolled off him onto her back and slipped her thumbs into the waistband of the panties and pushed them off over her legs. Then she directed Rick step by step through an extended session of foreplay before they embarked on a tour of what Bishop felt sure was every position from the illustrated edition of the *Kama Sutra*. Finally, Gabby whispered her permission for him to finish. He did, and then they collapsed in a sweaty, tangled mass of limbs and naked flesh, gasping for their breaths.

"Oh my, *rawr*, tiger," Gabby murmured. "As much as I'd hate losing Koko as a friend, you would be worth it. You're such a stud, baby. I can't get enough of you."

Bishop lay on his back, gasping for breath. He glanced at Gabby, also now naked, out of the corners of his eyes, and watched her voluptuous breasts rising and falling.

"How long do you intend to continue this until you feel you've had your revenge and we're even?" Bishop croaked.

"Mm, it isn't only about getting even, sweetie," Gabby chuckled. "I also like shagging you. So, I'm not sure I ever plan on it stopping."

Bishop groaned.

"I know you probably feel guilty for cheating on Koko, poor baby," Gabby said. "I'd never insist you break up with her. But you know, women can smell unfaithfulness a mile away. You know it's only a matter of time before you slip up, or she just figures it out that you're getting it on the side. Then you won't have to feel guilty about us anymore. Koko will decide for you."

"Come on, Gabby," Bishop pleaded. "This isn't right, not for any of us."

"Baby, you shouldn't play with fire unless you're prepared to get burned. You're the one that pursued me, remember?"

"It was only a little harmless flirtation between friends, Gabby. I never meant for anything like this to come of it."

"Mm, I don't remember it that way," Gabby said. "I seem to recall you actually begging for it that time even before the Big Island trip when I gave in, but you lost your nerve."

"I don't think you will tell Koko if I stop this," Bishop said petulantly. "It's bad enough you're betraying your friendship with Koko. I can't imagine you would intentionally hurt her by telling her about us. Please, can't we call it even now, and stop this before someone gets hurt?"

"I'm sorry, Rick. A woman wants what a woman wants. And you make me want you so bad, babe. You can't guilt me into giving it up. And, yes, I absolutely will tell Koko every excruciating detail if you force me to."

Bishop sighed, feeling dejected and hopeless. Gabby was right about one thing. It was only a matter of time before Koko got wise. He wasn't good at hiding his feelings from her, and every time this happened, he would feel guiltier and guiltier. Then Koko would interrogate him. And he'd break.

Gabby rolled toward him and groped him again.

"Gabby!"

"Once more, tiger, and I'll let you go until next time. I promise. And I see you want it as much as me. Come get your candy, baby."

CHAPTER TWENTY

Abigail's Plot

ABIGAIL STONE ROLLED OVER in bed and looked at Alex Baker snoring quietly beside her, his chest rising and falling. She had been sleeping with Alex on and off ever since they had met in Kabul when she had recruited him. After trying every trick in her formidable arsenal of seductive skills, Alex had not wavered on keeping a secret where he had stashed the money. That had not set well with Abby. She had been the architect of the $10 million heist and due the $5 million share she had demanded and her co-conspirators have agreed to. But so far, she hadn't gotten her hands on a dime of the money.

Abby Stone, as a CIA case officer in Kabul, had tired of watching everyone else getting rich from the rampant corruption, while all she had been getting was her monthly government paycheck. But then she heard about ten million coming into the city that the shit for brains activist woke politicians in Congress had appropriated to establish a gender studies program in a country largely run by extreme Islamic fundamentalists who were perfectly happy to continue living in the seventh century.

Five million was the seed money for the program, and the rainbows and unicorn farts crowd intended to use the other five million to pay bribes to selected corrupt faux-pro democracy Afghan government officials they needed to approve the establishment of the gender studies program. Of course, those officials were as much against the program as the Taliban. But they were more than happy to take the money of the idiot Americans. They had also known it was only a matter of time until the Taliban regained power and would roll back all the programs established by the naïve Western governments. So, supporting the ridiculous gender studies program would do no lasting harm. Abby understood all that and since the money would go to waste anyway, Stone saw her chance to get her piece of the fat corruption pie.

First, she did some basic intelligence work and learned the money would arrive at a naval finance facility where it would remain until the State Department disbursed it. Then she put out some feelers in the DOD contractor community, looking for some greedy operators willing to do the heavy lifting.

She found Mark Preston first, a natural fit for the operation. Preston was greedy and not opposed to taking part in a little criminal activity as long as the reward was worth the risk. Abby hadn't even had to sleep with him to get him on board. Preston recruited two of his buddies and then tried to recruit Baker. But Baker turned out to be a boy scout. He politely declined Preston's offer. They had to correct that since Preston had told Baker enough about the intended op that he posed a danger. Needing to pull him into the fold, Stone and Preston hatched a scheme by which Preston introduced her to Baker.

Abigail Stone wasn't vain about it, but she had realized at an early age that she had won the genetic lottery and was an uncommonly beautiful and desirable woman. Also, by the time she graduated high school, she had also figured out what made men tick and how she could easily manipulate them by using their natural, simple biological tendencies and urges against them. So, after they met, Abby unleashed her considerable feminine wiles on Alex Baker. By the second time they had slept together, he had become putty in her hands. He quickly changed his mind and agreed to help pull the heist.

The operation went flawlessly. They stashed the money, stacks of brand-new United States one-hundred-dollar notes, still shrink-wrapped, inside a shipping container that Preston had commandeered. Then he paid Petty Officer First Class Brian Greenwood, a navy logistics supervisor, ten thousand dollars to ship the container back to the States for him.

Preston, his two buddies, and Baker all returned to the States a few weeks later after their DOD contracts expired to await the container's arrival at an Army depot in Long Beach. However, Stone's tour got extended unexpectedly, leaving her stuck in Afghanistan for another month. That's when things went sideways.

First, a Navy cop arrested Greenwood on some unrelated charges when NCIS learned he had sold sensitive government equipment on the Kabul black market. Greenwood rolled over on Preston to strike a plea deal on his charges to get a reduced prison sentence. It hadn't taken the feds long to identify the other three DOD contractors who had helped steal the money. Then, once back home, Preston decided to cut both Baker and Abby out of their shares. Instead, he intended to split the money three ways with his original crew. Somehow, Baker got wise to Preston's plan. He beat the other three to the Army Depot, cleaned out the shipping container, and absconded with the entire $10 million.

When Abby finally got back to the States, she used her contacts at the agency to track down Preston and his crew. First, she discovered Preston's plan to rip her off. Then she learned Baker had gotten away with all the money. So, she promptly resigned from the CIA and began hunting Baker. That had been the simple part. Baker had already been looking for her. And when they reconnected, he promised to split the money evenly with her and she went on the run with Baker with former buddies chasing them.

Unfortunately, everywhere they went, Preston and company showed up. That went on for five long years. Then Greenwood got out of federal prison and joined in the chase after somehow learning about the $10 million while locked up. In desperation, she and Baker split up to throw their pursuers off their trail. Baker took the money with him, but that hadn't worried Abby. She knew he had fallen in love with her and wouldn't cheat her.

When Baker settled in Honolulu, where he had established a phony investment firm as cover, he reached out to Abby. She headed there to join him. But the Preston crew somehow followed her there and Greenwood followed them. Everyone had ended up in Honolulu.

Abby liked Alex, but had long since grown bored with him. Alex was a good dude, and while he wasn't great in the sack, he was okay. They had some good times. But no guy ever held her attention for long. Had it not been for the money, she would have dumped Alex long ago. Stone was confident Alex intended to share the money, but knew he had figured out she wouldn't stay with him once she got her half. Realizing that controlling the money was the only way he'd hang onto to her, Alex wasn't about to hand over her five million. And that just wasn't acceptable.

Abby decided as she lay there watching Alex sleep. She would get rid of him and keep the entire $10 million, or the $9 million and change that remained of it. And she had a plan.

Rick Bishop, the bumbling private detective, could help her accomplish her plan. She had seen how he had looked at her, almost salivating, like one of Pavlov's dogs. Abby felt sure luring Bishop into her web would be even easier than it had been with Alex. And he wasn't unattractive and was very fit. Abby doubted sleeping with him would be horrible. Then, once she had his loyalty, she would put Bishop on Alex's tail. That's what Bishop did for a living. He could follow Alex until he led Bishop to the money. Then she'd get her hands on the cash finally and could then eliminate Alex and Bishop. If Preston and his crew persisted and continued following her when she left Honolulu, then she would eliminate them, too, one by one. As soon as she and Alex arrived back in Honolulu, she would contact Bishop and put her plan into action.

CHAPTER TWENTY-ONE

The Tangled Web We Weave

BISHOP REVERSED OUT OF Gabby's driveway onto the street. As depressed as he felt, he smiled a little at the enormous oil slick the Toyota had left behind on her previously pristine driveway. She would probably need a power washer to remove it. As the Corolla's engine knocked and banged and backfired a time or two, Bishop drove toward his apartment thinking about the past four hours he'd spent with Gabby Inouye. She reminded him of the girl in the Matchbox Twenty song, *She's So Mean*. Gabby definitely fit the bill as a hardcore candy store, give me some more girl. And Bishop had never felt so miserable and hopeless with Gabby's threats hanging over his head. He hated himself, and his inherent weaknesses disgusted him. He had hopelessly mired himself in a trap he saw no way out of.

It appalled him he had even considered it briefly. But murder wasn't a realistic option, anyway. Was it? As a former homicide detective, he knew people rarely got away with murdering someone in their inner circle. And he knew scientific investigation techniques had grown ever more sophisticated since he'd left the cops. No, killing Gabby would never work unless he was willing to risk life in prison to escape her evil clutches. Bishop sighed. What was he going to do? What could he do?

Something had niggled at Bishop's brain for a while on and off, his comment to Greenwood about the sky being the limit at Joe's club as far as Brian working his way up the ladder to a better position. That comment reminded him of something Alex Baker had said to him, something Bishop had a gut feeling had been an important clue to the location of the stolen government money. Alex hadn't used the phrase the sky was the limit exactly when describing his business profit prospects, something that turned out to be farcical, but he had said something close to that. But with his raft of problems that defied resolution, Bishop couldn't quite pry the phrase from his overloaded memory banks. Something told him he would have to recall that phrase if he intended to find the money and collect the reward he hoped to get.

Bishop needed a shower. He could smell Gabby all over him. The close, stuffy interior of his old car reeked of the pungent odor of sex. Koko would get off work in less than two hours. There was no way Bishop could get cleaned up and prepare something for dinner before she got home. He needed a plan. And he couldn't forget about throwing his smelly clothes into the wash. Suspicious by nature, women weren't above digging through a dirty clothing hamper, seeking evidence of cheating, and Rick couldn't risk Koko doing that.

Arriving at the apartment, Bishop parked and rushed inside. He stripped off his clothes, jumped into the shower, and scrubbed himself until his skin felt raw. After taking his soiled clothing to the small laundry alcove off the kitchen, he tossed it all into the washer with soap and turned on the machine. Sure, the suit was dry clean only and washing it would ruin it, but that was a small price to pay. Having Koko detect Gabby's scents on the suit would cost Rick far more than paying for another gently used replacement at Goodwill.

Bishop dressed in clean boxers, a fresh shirt, and another suit. Then he combed his hair and checked his appearance in the bathroom mirror. Checking his watch, he saw he had less than an hour to get to the Likelike Club before Koko's shift ended.

Bishop stopped briefly at the office to see if Brian Greenwood was there. Rick had formed a desperate half-baked plan to extricate him from the hot mess he was in with Gabby. But Greenwood wasn't there. Bishop hoped that meant Joe had hired Brian and Greenwood was already working at the club. So, getting back in the Corolla, Rick motored, to use the term loosely, toward the Likelike.

When he arrived, Bishop went around back to the deck behind the club. There was still twenty minutes until Koko finished work, and he hoped to have a quick word with Brian. He lurked outside the door and peeked inside the bar. He saw no sign of Greenwood, but saw something that kindled his jealous anger. Kahiau Iona was sitting at the bar and Koko was leaning over the bar, smiling at him with her elbows on the bar and hands supporting her face. She seemed to hang on his every word, that is, when she wasn't giggling like a teenage schoolgirl. Even from his distant vantage point, Bishop saw Koko was flashing Iona a generous view of her impressive cleavage.

Rick hated Kahiau Iona. He and Koko had grown up in the same neighborhood and went to the same schools. While they had never dated, Bishop knew immediately the first time he met Kahiau from the way Iona looked at Koko that the guy was infatuated with her. And he spent an inordinate amount of time at the Likelike when Koko was working, flirting with her. Once, when Bishop had mentioned it to Koko, she laughed it off and told him to stop being silly and feeling so insecure. Kahiau was only an old friend from the hood.

Iona worked at a dive shop down at the marina and he was in Koko's circle of surfer friends. He went out of his way to find opportunities to spend time with her. Grudgingly, Bishop admitted Iona was an attractive guy. A brawny fellow who spent much of his time at the gym, Iona's muscular physique went beyond toned muscle structure and verged into defined, well-built curves. Even now, sitting at the bar, the muscles of his forearms, biceps, and chest strained against the fabric of his tight, black surfer's shirt.

Suddenly, Koko patted Iona's hand, nodded, and leaned over the bar to peck him on the lips. Then she took out her phone and turned away from the bar. Bishop started when his phone rang. He slunk away from the door and quickly dug out his phone. Since he had programmed a special ringtone for Koko, he hoped the conversation and music inside the club had muffled the ringtone, so Koko wouldn't realize he was standing right outside the bar. Punching the button, Bishop answered.

"Hey, babe," Koko said cheerfully. "You at home?"

"Almost," Bishop lied. "I had to stop by the office to pick up something. What's up?"

"Babe, Toni called in sick and Joe needs me to cover part of her shift. So just letting you know I'll be late getting home tonight. So go ahead and eat without me, okay?"

"Yeah, okay," Bishop said, hoping his tone hadn't revealed his suspicions.

"Okay, catch you later, babe," Koko said and then she disconnected.

That was interesting, Bishop thought. She hadn't even said "love you" as she did every time before ending a call with him. What the heck was going on? Bishop moved back to the doorway and peeked inside. Koko was leaning over the bar talking with Joe Rose and Joe looked uncomfortable. He glanced at Iona and then back at Koko and nodded. Then Koko removed her apron and tossed it on the counter behind the bar. Iona got to his feet as Koko made her way around the bar. They spoke, Koko giggled again, and then they walked out the front door of the bar together with Iona's hand on Koko's butt.

Brian Greenwood came out from the back through the double doors behind the bar, pushing a hand cart with a stack of cardboard boxes stacked on it. Greenwood parked the hand truck and begin filling the beer coolers from the boxes. Bishop still wanted a word with Brian, but now he wanted to talk with Joe first.

As Rick walked into the bar, he saw something else weird. Toni, the bartender that Koko said she was covering for, walked out of the back tying on her apron.

She glanced up, saw Rick, and smiled and waved. Bishop sat down on the stool next to Joe. Joe glanced at him.

"Hey, Richard," Joe said, before picking the folded newspaper beside him on the bar and pretending to read it with great interest.

"Hey, Rick," Toni said. "How's it going? The usual?"

"I'm doing okay, Toni," Bishop said. "And, yes, the usual. Thanks."

Toni nodded. "You got it." Then she reached into a cooler behind her and grabbed a Longboard Island Lager. After popping the top, she set the bottle on a coaster on the bar in front of Bishop.

"I heard you've been sick, Toni? You doing better?"

Toni laughed. "Sick?" she said. "Me? Who told you that? I'm right as the rain, Rick."

"I thought Koko mentioned it, but maybe I misunderstood."

"I guess so. I can't remember when I was sick last." Then Toni moved down the bar to wait on another customer.

Bishop sensed that his buddy Joe was nervous about something.

"Where's Koko?" he said innocently, curious to find out what Joe would tell him.

Rose cleared his throat. "Uh, well, she went off shift a minute ago," Joe said.

Bishop made a show of looking at the clock on the wall behind the bar.

"But it's not seven yet," he said.

"Uh, right. Well, Koko asked to leave a few minutes early and got Toni to come in to cover. I think she said something about a girl's night out."

"Did she? She didn't mention it to me. That's why I came by. I planned to take her to dinner. You know, to make amends for being so tied up with work lately."

Rose looked even more anxious. "Maybe she forgot to mention it," he said weakly.

"Joe, I know you're covering for her. So, why don't you spill it? Where is Koko really?"

Rose slowly folded the paper and put it back down on the bar.

"Richard, you're putting me in a tough spot. We're friends and go back a long way. But Koko is a friend too, and my business partner. And I don't really want to get in the middle of something that's none of my business."

"Joe!" Bishop growled. "Spill it. Tell me what you know."

"Oh, hell," Rose said. "Okay, Koko left a couple of minutes ago with Kahiau Iona."

"Left for where?"

"I think they are having dinner together or something. But I swear, Richard, I don't know where they went."

"Well," Bishop said, feeling his anger growing. "They have been friends for a long time. I guess there's nothing wrong with Koko having dinner with a friend."

Joe sighed. "I'm sure I'll regret this," he said stoically. "But do you remember when I told you the other day you needed to up your game if you wanted to hang on to Koko?"

"Yes," Bishop said cautiously.

"Well, here's the thing. Since you and Koko have been going through the rough patch, Kahiau Iona has spent a lot of time in the club. Even more time than usual. He has always flirted with Koko, but before she just sort of laughed it off. Now, she isn't laughing so much anymore."

"Are you telling me they left on a date?"

"Koko has been leaving early often lately, and leaving with Kahiau," Rose said. "I guess so she could spend time with him and still get home to your place around the usual time."

"What!" Bishop exclaimed. "That cheating slut! That bitch!"

"Calm down, Richard," Rose said it alarm. "I'm not saying they are shagging each other. But, yeah, they have been hanging out together a lot lately."

"You sure you don't know where they went?"

"No clue, Richard. Honest."

"Hey, Toni," Bishop said. "A Glenfiddich neat to go with my beer. Make it a double."

"You got it, Rick," Toni said.

A moment later, Toni set a glass of single malt whiskey on another coaster next to Rick's beer. Bishop tossed it down and asked for another.

"Richard, you aren't going back on the scotch, are you?" Rose said anxiously. "I thought you were past that. I can't recall when I last saw you drinking anything stronger than beer."

"Special occasion, Joe," Bishop growled, downing another glass of the Glenfiddich.

Greenwood returned with another cart load of beer boxes and noticed Bishop sitting at the bar.

"Rick, my man. How's it going, bud?"

"I'm okay, Brian. I see you landed the job."

"Yeah, and I love it here. Joe is a great boss."

"Thanks for bringing Brian around," Joe said to Bishop, desperate to change the subject. "You undersold him. With his Navy logistics skills, I hired Brian as assistant bar manager. He's taking over the inventorying and ordering to take a little off of Koko's plate."

"What time do you get off, Brian?" Bishop said.

"I was supposed to go off shift at seven, but I had a few things I wanted to finish up before heading out."

"See what I mean," Joe said. "Brian is a go-getter and a fast learner. I feel lucky to have him on the team."

"Okay, Brian," Bishop said. "When you finish work, I need to talk to you about something. But out on the deck where we don't have to shout over the music."

"Sure, Rick," Greenwood said. Then he grabbed the hand cart and took the empty boxes to the back.

"Richard, please give Koko a chance to explain things before you go off on her. I'm sure there must be a reasonable explanation. Maybe she just craved a little attention she wasn't getting from you, and Kahiau was available to provide it."

"Oh, you can count on it, Joe," Bishop said, waving his empty glass at Toni to signal he wanted a refill. "Koko has plenty of explaining to do."

Rick drank down the beer while he waited for Toni to pour him another scotch.

"That skank," Bishop muttered, slamming the empty bottle on the bar. "That cheating ho." His voice rose with every new insult he thought of to apply to Koko.

"Richard, calm down, please. Everyone is looking at you. And you're probably overreacting, anyway."

"Koko is boinking muscle boy behind my back, and I'm overreacting? Seriously, Joe?"

"We don't know that to be true," Joe said reassuringly.

"Don't defend that Mata Hari, Joe," Bishop growled, downing the whiskey Toni set on the bar.

Bishop's phone chirped. Taking it out, he looked at the text on the screen.

Off work but mom called. She needs to talk. It will be late so I'm going to sleep there tonight xo

Bishop laughed insanely. "Well, Joe, old buddy. I think we know it's true Iona is nailing her now. She says she won't make it home tonight."

"What!"

"Read it yourself, pal," Bishop said, tossing his phone on the bar.

"Well, she is off work and maybe she really is staying at her mom's house tonight."

"Knock it off, Joe. That's bull and we both know it. But if it makes you feel better, I'll call her mom later and ask to speak to her."

Greenwood came out of the back and walked around the bar.

"I'm finished, Rick," he said. "You wanted to talk?"

"Yeah," Bishop said, his voice now slurred. "Grab us a couple of beers and I'll meet you out on the deck. Tell Toni to put it on my tab."

"Okay, Joe," Bishop said, standing up unsteadily. "I'm going out on the deck to talk to my pal, Brian."

"All right, Richard," Rose said, holding out his hand. "But before you go let me hold your car keys. I don't want you getting behind the wheel. You're wasted."

"Whatever," Bishop said, pulling out his keys and dropping them in Rose's open hand. Then he staggered out of the bar onto the deck outside.

Brian came out a few moments later with two bottles of Longboard. He put one on the table in front of Rick and then sat down.

"Is this about me staying at the office?" Greenwood asked nervously. "I know it's an inconvenience, but I'll need to draw a couple of paychecks before I'll have money to get a place."

"Oh no, pal," Bishop said. "No problem with that. But I've been thinking. I have a sleeper sofa. How would you like moving in at my place until you get a place of your own?"

"Move in with you and Koko?" Greenwood asked with surprise.

"With me," Bishop said. "Koko isn't living there anymore. We're through."

"Uh-oh, sorry to hear that, bud. Did she find out about the pilot chick?"

"No," Bishop laughed drunkenly. "Turns out she's been banging some other dude behind my back. So, I'm dumping the slut."

"Huh. Well, sure, I guess it would be more comfortable staying at your apartment if you don't mind. But I swear just for a couple of weeks. Then I'll find a place."

"No worries," Bishop said. Then he guzzled down his beer. "Be a pal and grab us a couple more, huh?"

Brian nodded and returned to the bar for more beers.

CHAPTER TWENTY-TWO

Contact

THE HELICOPTER FLARED, DESCENDED, and then lightly touched down on the tarmac at the general aviation end of Honolulu International. Alex opened the door and jumped out. After lifting the luggage out of the back and setting it on the tarmac, he extended his hand to Abigail Stone. Taking it, she climbed down. Alex raised a hand to the pilot and shut the back door. Alex picked up the bags and then, bending at their waists, they hurried through the rotor wash towards the general aviation terminal. The couple walked inside and moments later, exited the front entrance. They stood together at the curb at the rental car shuttle stop. A man sitting on a bench down the way watched them surreptitiously from behind an open copy of *The New York Times*, the former newspaper, he was using to shield his face. A few minutes later, the shuttle arrived and stopped at the curb. Alex and Abigail got aboard and the shuttle pulled away. The man on the bench, folded and tossed the paper in a trash can where it belonged, and took out his phone.

"Smitty here," the man said. "Contact. Headed your way on the rental car shuttle."

"Terrific," Mark Preston said. "Jason is still watching the arrivals hall at the main terminal. Call him and tell him to meet me here at the car rentals facility and then drive over here."

"Okay," Smitty said, ending the call.

After calling Jason Logan and giving him the word, Smitty jogged to the parking lot and got into his gray rental. He reversed out of the parking space and drove towards the car rental facility. When he arrived, he pulled up next to the white sedan Preston had rented. They lowered their windows.

"Where's Jason?" Smitty asked. "I called and told him to get over here."

"He's inside watching them, to see which agency they rent from," Preston said.

Smitty nodded. "I have to hand it to you, Mark. You know how to run a surveillance op."

"Pretty simple stuff. They had to come through Honolulu International. I checked with all the helicopter services in Maui and they all said they landed here at general aviation. So, we had all the bases covered—the arrival hall for commercial flights, the general aviation terminal, and here in case they slipped by you guys."

"Now we just tail them to a hotel?"

"Yeah, we'll follow them and stake them out until Alex goes to pick up the money. Then we'll bag him and take it from him."

After Alex Baker and Abigail Stone came out of the car rental office, Jason Logan jogged to Preston's rental and got in the front seat.

"Cheap Rides," he said.

Preston nodded. "I can see their lot from here through these," Preston said, looking through a pair of binoculars. A few minutes later, he said, "Tan Hyundai two-door. They'll drive right past us to the exit, then we'll tail them."

Two minutes later, the tan Hyundai with Baker behind the wheel drove past. Preston dropped the binoculars in the seat and pulled out behind them, following them to the exit with Smitty bringing up the rear in his gray Ford rental.

Preston and his crew followed Baker and Stone until Baker pulled into the lot of an older hotel on Uluniu Avenue, the Royal Valley Resort Hotel.

"Doesn't look like much of a resort," Logan said as Preston stopped the car at the curb just short of the property.

"They tack resort onto the end of every hotel name on Waikiki so they can stiff the tourists for a resort fee," Preston laughed.

"I'm surprised they passed all the fancy places further down," Logan said. "I thought that Stone chick only traveled first class."

"They probably thought if we were in town waiting, we'd check all the luxe hotels," Preston said. "Alex figures he is outsmarting us by staying in a budget dump like this one."

"Except he didn't figure we would follow him right to it," Logan said with a laugh.

Smitty appeared at the window of Preston's rental.

"What now?"

"We make sure they check in," Preston said. "Then we'll rotate surveillance shifts, eight on and eight off. One of us will sleep back at the hotel while two of us watch with one guy sleeping and one guy staying awake."

"Why two? We got phones."

"Because they could split up, dummy."

"Ah, right. Didn't think of that."

"That's why you aren't in charge," Preston said.

When a valet got into the tan Hyundai and drove it into the parking garage, Preston felt satisfied Alex and Abby Stone had checked in.

"I've had the least amount of rack time lately," Preston said. "So, Logan, you and Smitty get the first watch. I'll relieve one of you in eight hours. If either of them leaves alone, one of you stays here on the hotel and the other follows the one leaving. I expect Alex to make the pickup, but you never know. So, we cover them both at all times."

"Okay," Smitty and Logan said in unison.

Logan got out and followed Smitty back to the gray Ford. Preston started his rental and drove off toward their hotel to get some sleep.

Less than an hour after they had arrived, Abigail Stone exited the front doors of the hotel wearing a hat and tight red dress and got into a taxi.

"Damn, I'd enjoy hitting that," Smitty said. "She is one desirable piece of ass."

"I hear you. She is that. But I heard back in the Stan she's a killer. Not sure I'd risk it."

Smitty laughed. "You got to live to a little dude. That just makes it more exciting. Now, sorry dude, but it's time to hop out. Stay on the hotel while I follow her."

"Yeah, yeah," Logan said, getting out of the car.

When the cab driver drove out of the lot into traffic, Smitty followed them away from Waikiki through the city into Chinatown until the taxi pulled over and stopped on Hotel Street. He stopped his rental near the end of the block behind the cab and watched as Stone got out. After glancing around, she walked directly across the street and entered a building. The taxi stayed put, apparently waiting.

Smitty got out and walked up the block until he found a spot in the shadows from which to watch the building. Then it occurred to him Preston would want to know where she went. So Smitty jogged across the street and read the painted print on the outside of the glass door that Stone had gone through. He chuckled, then turned and jogged back across the street to the position he'd left.

About fifteen minutes later, Stone exited the building, crossed the street, and got back into the cab. Once she was in the taxi, Smitty hurried back to the gray Ford and got in. Then he took off after the cab to make sure Stone was going back to the hotel.

CHAPTER TWENTY-THREE

Wasted Days and Wasted Nights

Hours earlier.

HOURS BEFORE SMITTY HAD had tailed Abigail Stone to his office, Bishop had awakened feeling tired and weak. His throat had felt dry and scratchy and he'd had a headache. His entire body had hurt and his temples had pounded. Rick had squinted against the sunlight streaming in through the open blinds of his bedroom window. Then realizing he still wore his clothes from the previous night except for shoes, and had laid on his bed with all the sheets and the comforter in a pile on the floor. Bishop had only vague recollections from the night before and hadn't remembered how he got home. One thing he had remembered was discovering that his girlfriend had been cheating on him behind his back. The alcohol he'd consumed had lessened the pain the night before, but recalling it all when he had awakened had felt like a gut punch.

Bishop had glanced at the clock on the bedside table, which had read 11:10. He'd assumed it was morning, given the sunlight. With a groan, he'd rolled out of bed and got up, but had then sat down quickly on the edge of the bed until the vertigo passed. Afterward, he had cautiously stood again and undressed, leaving his clothes on the growing pile on the floor. He'd stumbled to the bathroom, got into the shower, and had soaked under the hot water.

Bishop had drank two bottles of water from the frig before trying a cup of coffee. He'd found his phone on the kitchen bar. He had received three texts from Koko, all slightly different but with the same theme. "Did you get my text? Why are you not texting me back?" Clearly, she hadn't even come home to get dressed for work, which is where she would be after eleven in the morning. Rick had wondered if she would find out from Joe what had happened. He had felt sure Koko would have broken Joe as easily as he had the previous night. So, he had assumed Koko probably knew that he knew. Interestingly, he had received no texts from her except those from the previous night.

Bishop had found his car keys where he'd found the phone, put on his sunglasses, and had went out to the parking lot. He'd found the Toyota wasn't there, so had assumed it was still in the Likelike parking lot where he'd left it. So, he had called for a ride share to get to the office.

When the driver had dropped him in front of his office building, mercifully, Rick hadn't encountered Mrs. Wong. So, he had gone in the downstairs door and had taken the stairs up to his office. When he had entered, Brian Greenwood wasn't there, his cot and sleeping bag neatly folded and stored in the corner. Bishop had assumed Brian was also already at work. He had made another cup of coffee with the single serve brewer and had then sat down behind his desk. Bishop had just sat there alone, staring at the coffee cup with no expression in his eyes.

By one in the afternoon, the nausea had passed, and Bishop thought about going across the street to the Vietnamese restaurant to get lunch. As he got up and walked around the desk, the office door opened and Abigail Stone walked it, closing the door behind her. Bishop had thought her attractive the first they had met, but she looked like a million bucks now. Stone wore a red, light wool wide-brimmed sun hat that matched her red sleeveless body contouring dress that showcased all her feminine curves. Black stockings over her shapely, long legs and black patent leather heels completed the stunning ensemble.

For Bishop, Abigail's appearance was yet another wallop, a shock, and he barely drew a breath.

"Hello, Rick."

"Hello, Isla," Bishop said. "Of all the PI offices in all the world, you walk into mine."

Abigail smiled. "How nice. We share similar tastes in movies."

"What can I do for you, Ms. Stone?"

"Ouch, so formal. It's Abby, remember? Or you can keep calling me Isla if you like."

"Okay, Abby. What can I do for you?"

"I felt I owed you an apology, Rick," Abby said, looking at him tenderly. "Considering how we said goodbye last time."

"Ah, yes. I seem to recall a gun sticking in my back at the time. Well, what's one little gun among friends? Apology accepted."

Rick sat down in a visitor's chair in front of the desk, unsure what to do with his hands since the chair was arm-less. Abby strolled over to stand in front of him, still smiling.

"Anything else?" he asked.

"I want to hire a private investigator, actually."

"Well, you're in luck. You walked right into a private investigator's office. However, I'm pretty busy and not looking for another client at the moment."

"That busy, are you? Too busy to help a needy old friend?"

"Well, like they say, a friend in need is a friend indeed."

Abby took off her hat and laid it on the desk behind her, along with her clutch purse. Then she turned back to Bishop, and lifted the hem of the short, tight dress well above her waist, exposing her black garter belt and black lace thong panties. Stepping forward, she straddled Bishop's legs and lowered herself onto his lap. Then she took his face in her hands and kissed him. As the kiss went on, a lot of tongue action became involved as Abby sensually ground her crotch against Bishop's. Always the gentleman, he rose to the occasion.

When Abby broke the kiss and leaned back, they were both a little breathless.

"Will that do for a retainer?" she asked with a mischievous grin.

"I think we're getting there," Bishop said hoarsely.

"Mm, well, I'm not a girl who likes getting it while sprawled on a desk," she said. "But maybe I could come by your apartment later and offer you a bit more."

"That would be swell," Rick said. "But where is Alex?"

"He's at the hotel," Abby said. "We arrived from Maui late this morning and he's resting. I told him I had a few errands to run."

"I don't suppose you'll tell which hotel?"

"Not yet," Abby said with a flirtatious smile. "But I might tell you later if you play your cards right."

"Sure, I suppose I'm intrigued now," Bishop said. "Shall we say around seven?"

"Perfect," Abby said, kissing her long index finger and pressing it to Bishop's lips. After Rick gave her the address, she squirmed off his lap, and standing, she pulled her dress back down. After putting on her hat and picking up her purse, she looked back at Bishop. "See you at seven then, handsome." Then she strolled back toward the door with plenty of sensual hip action, opened it, and went out.

"Good lord," Bishop sighed. "There goes a woman."

Stiffly, he stood up and walked to the window facing the street and looked down. A moment later, Abby emerged from the building. After checking the traffic, she strolled across the street to a taxi at the curb, got into the backseat, and the cab pulled away. Then, Bishop saw someone else he recognized, one of Preston's men who had been lurking in the shadows across the street. He hot-footed it toward a gray sedan parked further up the street. Abby had a tail.

Bishop flew through the door, not bothering to lock it, and took the stairs two at a time. He burst through the downstairs door and sprinted across the street. But as he hurried along the sidewalk toward the gray car, the driver pulled out into traffic before he got to it. Another taxi rounded the corner and drove toward him. Frantically, Bishop flagged it down, and the taxi whipped in next to the curb. Rick jumped into the backseat.

"Follow that gray Ford," he said, pointing at the sedan ahead.

The driver turned and looked at him incredulously. "Are we in a movie?"

"No," Bishop said, shoving a fifty in the driver's face. "Drive before we lose him?"

Snatching the fifty, the driver said, "Okay, bruddah." He dropped the car into gear and shot into traffic.

"Keep it in sight, but don't get too close," Rick said.

"You got it."

Time to follow the money, Bishop thought.

The taxi continued straight back to the hotel, stopping nowhere else, and dropped Stone off at the front doors.

Smitty drove past, made a U-turn and parked at the curb across the street where he'd dropped off Jason. Logan opened the door and got back in the front seat.

"Where did she go?" he asked.

"To see that private eye we ran into on Maui. Bishop."

"Huh? What's up with that, dude?"

Smitty shrugged. "Beats me. But I'll tell you what. It wouldn't surprise me if Stone is working on a plan to cut Baker out of the deal and keep the money herself."

"You think?"

"Makes as much sense as anything. Otherwise, why is she going to see Bishop alone?"

Abby smiled at her reflection in the mirrored wall inside the elevator as it rose to the fourth floor where the room was. She carefully reapplied her smeared lipstick. Bishop would be easier than she had expected. He had wanted her desperately after the little lap dance. Somehow, she would convince Alex to go get dinner alone without her. Maybe she would tell him she wasn't feeling well. Then, after he left the hotel, she would grab a taxi and head to Bishop's apartment. Of course, it would piss off Alex, but if Bishop was any good the first time this evening, she might even spend the night there.

CHAPTER TWENTY-FOUR

What to Do

BISHOP'S TAXI CAUGHT UP with the gray sedan and Abby's cab before it turned off Uluniu Avenue and stopped in front of the Royal Valley Resort Hotel. Bishop watched Abby get out and walk into the lobby. The gray Ford made a U-turn and then pulled up at the curb across the street from the hotel. As Bishop's cab drove by, he saw a second man, not Preston, getting into the Ford with the other guy.

"Go a block further, then do a U-turn and pull over to the curb," Bishop said. "I need to monitor that car until I figure something out."

"I've got to keep the meter running," the driver said.

"Don't worry," Bishop said. "The fifty is for you. I'll pay the fare on the meter."

"Now you're talking, bruddah."

"What to do?" Bishop asked himself. Now he didn't need Abby Stone any longer because he knew where Alex was. One option was he could retrieve his car and come back and set up and watch for Alex to go to pick up the money. But he couldn't be sure Alex and Abby would go together. They might split up as a diversion. Then he couldn't be sure which would make the pickup. And he needed to get rid of Preston and his crew. He wouldn't be able to take them all on, all alone. Then he got an idea.

Bishop took out his phone and saw he had four missed calls from Koko, but only one voicemail. He would deal with that later. Rick called NCIS Special Agent Bob Utley at Pearl. Utley came on the line.

"Got something, brother?" he said.

"Yeah, I have eyes on two of them sitting in a gray Ford sedan on Uluniu Avenue across from the Royal Valley Resort Hotel," Bishop said. "I haven't seen Preston, but I expect he is close by."

"Hang on a second, Rick," Utley said. "Let me get some agents on the way to you."

Utley put him on hold and came back on the line about three minutes later.

"Okay, I've got four agents leaving Pearl right now. Can you maintain surveillance?"

"Yeah, I'll hang out until they get here. But tell them not to spare the horses. I'm paying a cabbie for waiting time."

"It shouldn't take them long," Utley said. "Why do you think they are watching the Royal Valley Resort Hotel? Alex Baker staying there?"

"Yes, I saw Abigail Stone, the fifth member of the team, walk into the lobby two minutes ago. But listen, Bobby, you can't take Alex and Stone down until we find the money. If you arrest them, neither of them will tell you squat. They will go to jail if they have to and wait it out and get the money later."

"But we're good to go on the other three?"

"That's up to you, brother," Bishop said. "But if you take these two right away, they may not tell you where to find Preston. If it were me, I'd set up surveillance and wait until Powers shows up. He's the boss, at least of these two. I'm sure he'll show, eventually."

"Yeah, I fully support that idea," Utley said. "All right, I'm not coming out. I'll wait to hear from you and I'll tell the agents to set up on those two suspects and then to standby until Powers shows."

"Sounds good," Bishop said. He described the taxi he was in and how to find him.

"Okay, I'll have my guys contact you discreetly so you will know when they are on the scene."

"Great," Bishop said. Then he and Utley rang off.

"Should only be a few more minutes," Bishop said to the driver. "I've got some help on the way to watch the car. Then I'll need you to drive me somewhere."

The driver nodded.

Bishop checked his voicemail and listened to Koko's message. While he'd been on the phone with Utley, there had been another missed call from her and she had left another message. He listened to the first one.

"Um, hey, babe. You're not returning my calls or replying to texts. Look, may I come to the apartment after work? We really need to talk, okay? Let me know, please. I'm here until seven. Thanks."

Bishop took a deep breath. That confirmed everything. Joe had told her he knew about her affair with Iona. Otherwise, she wouldn't have felt the need to ask his permission to come to the apartment to talk. Usually, it had been Bishop that had initiated the breakups with past girlfriends. Or he'd at least purposely provoked them to end things when he felt the relationships had no longer worked. But as far as he knew, at least, none of those women had ever cheated on him. Koko was the last woman he would have ever expected to do it. But maybe all women were capable of it under the right circumstances. Bishop took another deep breath and then listened to the second message she'd left.

"Hey. I can imagine how angry and hurt you must feel. Rick, I'm not trying to put it on you. It was my mistake. But I missed you. I was lonely without you and couldn't cope. You worked all the time and left me alone so much. I was weak, and that's no excuse because I knew it was wrong. Last night, I only wanted to end it with him, hoping you would never find out. I swear. Anyway, please see me and let's talk. I don't want it to end like this. Please, Rick. Call me."

Bishop sighed, turned the phone off and put it into his pocket. He wiped his eyes. Damn, it really hurt. But didn't he deserve every bit of the pain? He knew he was feeling what Koko would have felt if she had learned about his affair with Gabby. Even if she found out about it now after what she had done, she'd probably still feel angry and hurt, just as he did now. How could he be angry at Koko when he'd done the same thing to her? Last night that had never even occurred to him. But he thought about it now. Bishop started when someone tapped on the window glass. It was a young woman in a business suit. Bishop cracked the door.

"Richard Bishop?" the woman asked.

"Yes."

"I'm Special Agent Phillips with NCIS. We're set up on the gray Ford, sir. You can leave the area now."

"Great, Agent Phillips," Bishop said. "Good luck."

Phillips nodded and walked away.

Bishop shut the door and told the driver to take him to the Likelike Club. He turned his face away as they passed the gray sedan.

CHAPTER TWENTY-FIVE

Inspiration Strikes

BISHOP HAD TOLD THE cabbie to drive him to the Likelike Club so he could pick up his car. When they arrived, Rick paid the fare and then got into the Toyota. He had received three more missed calls from Koko, but no voicemails. But he wasn't ready to talk to her yet. Maybe later, but not now. Bishop wasn't sure what he'd say and needed time to think. So he cranked the beast and drove out of the lot towards his apartment. It was on his way there that the mental tumblers finally clicked and fell into place. He remembered what Alex Baker had said that day about his business profits.

"Profits are literally going through the roof."

Rick felt sure he now knew where Alex had stashed the money. It was so simple he couldn't believe he hadn't thought of it before. Especially when he had figured out that Alex hadn't had the money with him in Maui.

When Rick got to the apartment, he called another friend, his former partner, at HPD.

"Lieutenant Chang, Criminal Investigations. How can I help you?"

"David, it's me."

"Hello, Richard," Chang said cautiously. "I hope you aren't calling to ask a favor. We've already settled that and so far you've kept your word."

"Actually, I am calling to ask a favor, but David, you're really going to want to get in on this one."

"Somehow, I doubt that, Richard. What do you want?"

"First, I need you to put some patrol officers outside of an office downtown to make sure no one enters it. Then I need you to go somewhere with me as an official witness," Bishop said. "Oh, and I need you to arrange to bring a fire engine along."

There was silence on the line.

"David? You there?"

"Richard, I ran into Joe Rose. He told me your were hitting the booze again. I hoped because of the circumstances Joe mentioned, it was only a temporary relapse. But, Richard, as a friend, maybe you need to get professional help this time."

"David, I'm not drunk. This is serious. I'm talking about a big heist of $10 million that the FBI and NCIS haven't been able to crack for over five years. Think of the positive publicity the department and you, David, will get from helping blow this case wide open. You might make captain out of this."

"Richard, for the sake of argument, if I was interested in any of that, I can't just drop everything to come over and help you with one of your crazy cases."

"You thought I meant right now? Oh no, David. What do you take me for? All I need immediately is the patrol officers to secure the office I mentioned. I don't need you to do anything else until tomorrow. I have a loose end to tie up first."

"Where is it you want me to go with you?"

"The same office I'm talking about, downtown. I'm sure there is stolen government money there and I need you there as an official witness when we recover it?"

"Richard, as I understand this, it's a federal case, right? So I don't see HPD having any jurisdiction. We can't get a search warrant because you've given me no grounds. You haven't even told me of any crime committed that we have jurisdiction over. And I'm certainly not going to accompany you on a break and entering or take part in an illegal search."

"I swear it is all completely legal, David," Bishop said, picking up his key ring and flipping through the keys. There on the ring was the key Baker had given him to his office the day Alex asked him to release Greenwood from the locked closet. "The tenant of the property voluntarily gave me a key so I can legally enter the premises whenever I want. You don't have to do anything but show up as an official witness."

"Except expend department resources guarding the premises overnight, and provide the fire engine and personnel you mentioned."

"Well, yes, that. But except for the overnight watch, we're not talking much in the way of resources. We won't tie up the fire department long at all. I promise. And I think I can get the feds to reimburse HPD for the patrol resources."

Chang sighed loudly. "Richard, this better all be on the level."

"It is, David. I swear it. Will you help me?"

"All right, Richard, I'll consider it, against my better judgement. But I want to hear all the details before I decide."

"That's fair," Bishop said. Then he gave Chang a quick summary of the entire story, beginning with the heist in Kabul.

"Why can't the feds handle what you're asking me to do?" Chang asked when Bishop finished the summary.

"There's a lot of moving parts, David, and other aspects of the investigation are requiring all their resources." Bishop figured telling Chang about his plan to collect the $2 million reward part wouldn't help his case. So, he didn't mention it.

"All right, I'll put patrol outside the door, but not past noon tomorrow. Can you tie up your loose end by then so we can finish the rest of it?"

"Yes, that's perfect, David. If you could get someone out there by six this evening, we'll wrap it all up by noon tomorrow at the latest."

"All right, give me the address."

Bishop gave it to him and then thanked Chang profusely for helping. "I'll call you tomorrow morning by ten and we can organize the last part of it."

Chang sighed again. "All right, Richard. Call me."

Saying he'd just walk to the burger place down the block and bring back takeout, Alex finally left the room after six o'clock. Abby had told him she had an upset stomach and didn't want to go out for dinner. She listened with her ear to the door until she heard the ding of the elevator arriving down the hall. Then she waited a beat before frantically stripping off her clothes and jumping into the shower, careful not to get her hair wet. After showering, she quickly applied tasteful makeup and brushed her hair.

She then selected a tight black tank and a shamefully short mini-skirt from her wardrobe.

"That should get Bishop's attention," she said aloud, and giggled while putting on a hot pink bra and panty set.

Leaving the room, Abby pushed the call button for the elevator, hoping she got outside the hotel without running into Alex returning to the room. There was no way he would believe she was running an errand dressed like a call girl.

Just as she pushed out through the front doors, something caught her attention and she drew back. It was a car parked across the street diagonally from the hotel. It was the same gray sedan she remembered seeing on Hotel Street earlier. She was sure of it. Abigail Stone, formerly of the Central Intelligence Agency, noticed things like that. Peering out the glass door, she saw the front seat passenger get out and stretch. Then he lit a cigarette and turned to face her. The man was Jason Logan, one of Preston's crew. Somehow, they had found them and were waiting for Alex to lead them to the money. But she would worry about that later.

Abby hurried through the lobby to the side door that exited out to the pool area. Outside, she skirted the pool and took the concrete steps down to the beach at the back of the hotel. On the bottom step, she paused and removed the heels she had on, and carrying the shoes in her hand, she walked down the sandy beach to a neighboring hotel. After leaving the beach, she put the shoes back on and walked through the hotel lobby and out the front doors. There she asked a doorman to hail a taxi for her.

A few minutes later, a cab drove up in front of the hotel. The doorman opened the back door and Abby got in. After she gave the driver the address, he nodded and pulled out onto the street. Abby sank back against the seat and looked at her phone to check the time. The screen read 6:38. Good, she thought with relief. She'd make it there by seven.

At a little before seven, Bishop heard a knock at the front door. He knew who it was. He'd given Abby Stone the actual address of his apartment earlier that day. And they had made a date for seven that evening. But at the time, Rick had intended to use Abby to find Alex Baker. Now he didn't need her any longer. He already knew the hotel Alex was staying in with Abby. And since the memorable meeting in the visitor's chair in his office, Bishop had also formed a compelling theory about where Alex had stashed the $10 million. So, Bishop didn't even need Baker any longer.

Earlier, he'd decided he wouldn't bother answering the door when Abby arrived. But by the time seven rolled around, he'd changed his mind. The more he'd thought about it, the more the idea had appealed to him to have a little fun at Abby's expense. He'd caught the momentary look of smugness and contempt in her eyes when she had ended the kiss and leaned back while sitting on his lap with her dress pulled up around her perfect hips. Abby had believed he was an easy mark for her seductive skills. But he'd only gone along with it as part of his plan to get to Alex Baker through her. Well, mostly. She believed she'd had Bishop eating from her hand, but she'd been so wrong about that. Well, sure, she had excited him a little. But Rick accepted he was only human and his response had been involuntary. Was there a red-blooded guy anywhere who could have withstood Abby's salacious, lubricious onslaught without at least a slight physical response? Bishop felt confident he had held his own. Frankly, he was curious to know more about what plan Abby had devised that she wanted to use him as a pawn in and how far she would go to get what she wanted from him. So, when the second knock came, this time more insistent, Rick walked to the door and opened it. Standing outside it was Abigail Stone.

Abby was what every woman would want to be. She was tall and athletic looking with thick dark hair expensively styled. Instead of the body-hugging red dress from earlier, Abby had on after-six casual wear—a tight black tank with spaghetti straps over an ultra-short aqua wrap around mini skirt. The hem barely concealed the gap where the tops her long silky legs joined her torso. She wore strappy, open-toed five-inch heels with the outfit. With so much of her tempting body displayed, Bishop saw Abby sported an even tan, which didn't appear precancerous, and had the advantage of reminding him she spent a great deal of time on the beach. She looked like she belonged in health club ads.

"Hello, Rick. May I come in?"

"Yes, please do," Bishop said, standing to the side to allow her to strut confidently on her heels into the apartment living room. Bishop closed the door.

"A drink?" Bishop said. "Coffee?"

"A beer would be nice if you have any."

"I have Longboard Island Lager in the frig," Bishop said.

"That's fine," Abby said, as if it made a difference, while settling herself on the living room sofa.

Bishop returned from the kitchen with beers and handed Abby a bottle and a glass before sitting down at the opposite end of the sofa. She set the glass on the coffee table and put the bottle to her smiling, succulent lips, and drank some beer. Then she stretched like a cat, shifted to lean back against the arm of the sofa, and kicked off her heels before swinging her legs up and putting her feet in Bishop's lap. Her movements forced the hem of the short skirt dangerously higher, revealing a hint of the hot pink panties beneath. Bishop glanced down as the perfectly manicured, polished toes of one bare foot seductively caressed the inside of his thigh. The nail polish, also hot pink, matched her underwear. He gulped some beer and then looked up into Abby's smiling eyes. Her body seemed restless under the clothing, brief as it was, as if her natural state was naked, and clothes only a grudging nod to decency. Abby smiled, moistened her lips with her tongue, and sipped more beer from the bottle. There was a faint dreamy quality about her, as though she were always a little disengaged, thinking of her gorgeous body and its effect on men.

"Shall I tell you why I want to hire you?" Abby said. "Or do you wish to collect the balance of the retainer first?"

Bishop didn't like the glib way she had suggested they have sex. It was as if for her it was a foregone conclusion that he'd figuratively jump at the chance to literally jump her bones. And once he had tasted it, he'd do anything she asked to get more. Rick smiled graciously, the civilized gumshoe, but declined the offer.

"I'd like to hear more about what it is you would like me to do first," he said.

Abby pushed her bottom lip forward as if to express petulant annoyance, but it was more to make herself look even more sexually attractive, Bishop figured. He surreptitiously slipped his left hand beneath a couch pillow and switched on the micro-recorder he'd stashed there earlier.

"Talk is boring, but all right," Abby said in a faux-whiny tone. "We returned to Honolulu so Alex could pick up the money," she said. "But I've concluded he doesn't intend to give me my $5 million share."

"Why would he hold out on you?"

"Because he wants to hold on to me. I'm bored with Alex and have been for a long while. Unfortunately, he knows it and knows I'll leave him if I got my cut."

"Your cut?" Bishop said. "That smacks of entitlement. I thought Alex was only sharing his money with you because you're together."

"Alex and I are not a couple," Abby said. "We never were. Yes, you could say we've shared a friends with benefits arrangement when we've not been with others. And of course, I'm entitled to half the money. The heist was my idea. I planned it and then recruited the men from the DOD contractor community to do the heavy lifting. But they all turned out greedier than I'd expected and irritating circumstances have thus far frustrated my attempts to get what is rightfully mine."

"What is it you intend for me to do?"

"If we can come to an agreement, I will tell you where to find Alex and I want you to tail him when he goes to pick up the money from where he has hidden it. Then I want you to take the money from Alex and give it to me."

"Your half?"

"No, we're well past sharing now," Abby said. "After all the double-crossing and backstabbing I've endured, I want all of it."

"Just a thought, but Alex might object to me taking the money from him."

Abby smiled. "You're a big, tough, smart guy. I'm confident you will figure something out."

"Someone could get killed. Ten million is a lot of money."

Abby sighed. "It's so stuffy and warm in here," she said, setting her bottle on the coffee table. Then, crossing her arms and grabbing the hem of the tight tank with her fingers, she pulled it up and off over her head and dropped it on the floor. She had on a strapless push-up bra underneath of the same hot pink color as her nails and panties. The bra compressed her magnificent, munificently sized breasts so severely that evenly tanned mounds of flesh welled from the top of the bra, threatening to pop free. Abby stood, untied the skirt, and, unwrapping it, allowed it to drop to the floor. Then she glided over and dropped onto the couch beside Bishop, nuzzling and tenderly kissing his neck.

"I'm bored with talking, handsome. Can't we relax and have some fun now?"

Bishop groaned inwardly, cursing his weakness. Things were not going at all as he had planned now that he had a woman with the most perfect body he'd ever seen, clad only in a bra and string bikini panties pressed against him. Abby deftly unbuttoned his shirt and then planted soft kisses on his chest as her nimble fingers went to work on his belt and trousers. To Bishop, it seemed only mere seconds had passed before he was sitting on the couch wearing only his boxers while Abby, now braless, reclined in his lap with her arms around his neck, kissing him deeply, her tongue seeking his.

Abby shifted off his lap, stood, and took hold of Bishop's legs and swung them onto the sofa. Then, with him lying supine, her thumbs inside the waistband of his boxers, she pulled them down and off. She then put her thumbs inside the waistband of her bikini panties and was slowly and salaciously slipping them down over her breathtaking thighs when Bishop heard someone inserting a key in the lock at the front door.

"Uh-oh!" Bishop said aloud, without intending to. His excitement wilted, he sprang up and desperately searched the floor for his boxers as the front door swung open. Abby glanced back over her shoulder just as her hot pink panties hit the floor around her ankles. Both Rick and Abby saw a clearly astonished Koko framed in the front doorway, her eyes wide and open-mouthed.

CHAPTER TWENTY-SIX

Women Scorned

HER WIDE BROWN EYES flashing daggers and her nostrils flared, Koko dropped the hand from her mouth.

"Richard Bishop!" she cried. "You bastard! What's this? Revenge sex with an escort, no less? Seriously?"

"Hey, I'm no escort, bitch!" Abby cried defensively, covering her breasts with hands crossed at the wrist, but not effectively. "And who the hell are you?"

"His girlfriend!" shouted Koko, pointing a long accusing finger at Bishop.

Abby glanced at Bishop. "What?" she gasped. "Girlfriend?"

Bishop grinned sheepishly, now sitting on the couch with his hands covering his crotch.

"Remember when I mentioned the surfer girlfriend?"

"You said she died in a surfing accident! She seems very much alive to me."

"Well, by nature, I'm a storyteller and sometimes am given to embellishment," Bishop said. "Koko had a surfing accident, but maybe I exaggerated the dead part a little."

"You told her I was dead!" Koko screamed.

"What did she mean, revenge sex?" Abby said, recovering her wits slightly.

"Oh, yeah!" Bishop said, springing from the couch and turning the finger of accusation on Koko. "She's not my girlfriend anymore. She has been screwing some muscle-bound surfer dude behind my back!"

Koko turned, moving her finger to Abby and said, "Get dressed and then get the hell out of my house, slut!"

"I was here first!" cried Abby. "You get the hell out. Rick just said you're not his girlfriend anymore."

"Calm down," Bishop said, shimmying into the boxers he'd finally found beneath the edge of the sofa. "Both of you settle down." Fearing the women were about to come to blows, he wanted to de-escalate the situation.

Crossing her arms, Koko said defiantly, "I'm not going anywhere."

After noticing that Bishop was putting his clothes back on, Abby started picking up her discarded articles of clothing and putting them on. It didn't seem the best time to be the only naked person in the tension-filled room.

"You could have at least talked to me first, you bastard," Koko said to Bishop. "I've called and texted you all day long."

Bishop held up his open hands in surrender. "There's nothing to discuss," he insisted. "You may choose whoever you want to sleep with. And so can I. I wish you and that damn muscle head all the best and hope he makes you happy."

"Rick, I made a horrible mistake," Koko wailed. "I already broke it off with Kahiau. I love you and came here to apologize and to try to salvage our relationship. Then I walk in and you're already boning some slut in our living room."

"It sounds like you're the slut around here, skank," Abby retorted, "so you can knock it off with the pejoratives directed at me."

"Technically, I wasn't boning her," Bishop pointed out. "Things hadn't gone that far when you busted in."

Koko rolled her eyes at Bishop. "Who the hell is she, anyway?" she demanded.

"Oh, forgive me," Bishop said. "Where are my manners? Abigail Stone, meet Koko Mahelona, my ex-girlfriend. Koko, meet Abigail Stone, a potential client."

"Charmed, I'm sure," Abby said dismissively.

"Pfft," said Koko. "Client? Is she paying you with sex?"

"What if I am?" said Abby. "Is that any of your business?"

"Enough," Bishop said, now fully dressed again. Crossing the floor to Koko, he tried to usher her gently back out the still open door.

"Koko, please go to your mom's place. I'll call you later and we can meet if you still want to talk. But now isn't the time."

"Why should I leave?" Koko said, jerking away from Bishop's hands. "Do you and the slut want to pick up where you left off when I interrupted?"

"It's all over," Bishop said. "I'm calling a taxi for Abby and she is leaving too."

"We have business to discuss," Abby argued.

"Please, Koko," Rick pleaded. "Please go."

"Fine," Koko said. "Don't bother calling. I have nothing I want to talk about with you. Not ever." Then she turned and stormed out.

"She's insane," Abby said. "Now shut the door so we can talk."

Bishop watched Koko striding to her car and then speeding out of the parking lot. Without turning, he said, "I meant what I said. You're leaving too, Abby. The party is over and I'm calling you a taxi."

Closing the door, Bishop went to the kitchen counter and picked up his phone. Then he called a taxi service while Abby sat on the sofa frowning with her arms crossed. Crossing the floor to the window so he could watch for the taxi, Bishop said, "I can't help you, Abby."

"You mean you won't help me? Is that what you're saying?"

"Okay, I won't," Bishop said. "I already know where Alex is. More importantly, I know where the money is and I'm returning it to the government. You and Alex should forget the money and leave Honolulu if you still can. The feds know you're here and they are already looking for you both."

Abby jumped to her feet. "Maybe they are looking for Alex, but not me. They have nothing on me."

Bishop's phone rang, and he looked at the screen.

"Hold that thought," he said. "I need to take this." Then he answered the call.

"Rick, Bob here," Utley said. "We got them. Powers showed up to relieve one of his guys, and my team took them all down. They are booking them into FDC Honolulu as we speak. And we're maintaining surveillance on the Royal Valley Resort Hotel. Baker and Stone won't be able to leave without us seeing it."

Bishop grinned, figuring Abby must have slipped out before NCIS was in place fully. "Remember our deal?" Bishop said. "It's important."

"About not taking down Baker and Stone until you give me the word about the money?"

"Yes, and I should have something for you by noon tomorrow."

"Then yes, I'm still tracking on that. We'll just continue the surveillance and stay on them if either or both of them leave the hotel. But we won't move in until I hear from you."

"Great, Bob. Thanks for trusting me with this. You won't regret it."

"I'm not worried, brother. You stay safe, yeah?"

"Always," Bishop said, ending the call.

"What was that all about?" Abby said, clearly suspicious.

"Something I'm helping a guy with," Bishop said. "There's the taxi."

He walked to the door and opened it. Abby got up from the sofa and walked over. Pausing at the door, she looked into Bishop's eyes.

"You have no idea what you just missed out on," she said.

"I think I can imagine," Bishop said. "You're a very desirable woman, Abby. But now you should know something. The feds have arrested Powers and his crew. If they have nothing on you as far as your connection to the heist, I expect that will soon change. Tell Alex what I said. It's time to forget the money and run."

Abby paled, and her mouth dropped open. Then she turned and hurried out to the waiting taxi. Bishop watched her from the doorway until she got in the back seat of the cab.

"Yes," Bishop said with a deep sigh of regret. "I'm pretty sure I can imagine what I missed out on, Abigail Stone."

.

Chapter Twenty-Seven

Frustration

THE TAXI DROPPED ABBY Stone in front of the Royal Valley Resort Hotel. Glancing across the street, she saw the gray sedan was no longer there. Bishop had told her the truth, it seemed. And that was a good thing. At least she and Alex no longer had to worry about Mark Preston and his crew. But the rest of what Bishop had told her wasn't good news. It wasn't good news at all. Abby was feeling panicked. Not that she wasn't worried about the feds connecting her to the Kabul heist. But what worried her the most was never getting her hands on that money. She would have to convince Alex they had to pick up the money right away. Seeing nothing else suspicious, Abby turned and walked into the lobby and took the elevator up to the room.

When she let herself in with her key card, Alex immediately started in on her. He ranted like a spoiled little boy forced to share his favorite toy. She crossed her arms and stared at him, letting him rage and get it out of his system.

"Shut up, Alex!" she said finally when it seemed he'd never stop. "That's enough."

"Where have you been, Abby?"

"I went out for a while."

Baker glared at her. "Dressed like that? Like a common streetwalking whore?" he spat.

Abby slapped him hard across the face.

"Don't ever speak to me like that again, Alex," she said. "I'm not your property, so stop this jealous boyfriend nonsense right now. I don't need your permission to go out. And I don't answer to you. And I will damn well dress as I please."

Baker stood with his hand to his cheek where she had slapped him, his puppy dog eyes filled with hurt.

"I was worried," he said. "I need to trust you, Abby, and you taking off without a word after I've left the room doesn't make me feel warm and fuzzy."

"If you've calmed down, I'll tell you where I went and why. I've learned something you need to know so we can make plans."

"Okay, I'm calm," Baker said, sitting on the bed, looking defeated and hurt. "I called Bishop, and I went to a bar nearby and had a drink with him."

"Bishop? Why?"

"When I went out to run errands earlier, I thought I saw a gray sedan following the taxi," Abby said. "Later, when I went downstairs to the pool, I looked out the lobby exit doors and saw the same car parked across the street."

"Someone has us staked out?" Alex said with alarm, temporarily forgetting his jealousy.

"Preston's crew," Abby said. "One of them got out of the car to smoke and I recognized him."

Baker's eyes widened. "Preston found us?"

"Obviously. So, I started thinking, and I thought of Bishop. He's a private investigator, so it made sense he knows people in local law enforcement. It made sense he could help get Preston off our tails if I could only convince him to do it."

"Well, why didn't you tell me about seeing Preston's crew? Why did you sneak away while I was gone to get dinner?"

"Alex, do you think I didn't notice in Maui how jealous you were of Bishop? I didn't tell you because I didn't want the drama. I knew you would act just as you did when I walked in here five minutes ago. That's why I slipped away and took care of everything the way I did."

Baker took a deep breath, and his shoulders sagged.

Abby continued. "Because of how we left things with Bishop in Maui, I knew he wouldn't be eager to help us. So, yes, I put on a sexy outfit after I persuaded him to meet me for a drink to talk. I used the assets I have to get a conversation started and then to persuade him to help us."

"Did you..." Alex began, but his voice trailed off.

"I can't believe you even asked me that, Alex?" Abby said, feigning anger. "And no, I did not! I only let him have an eyeful, flirted a little with him, and then made some promises I certainly won't keep. But that was enough to encourage him to agree to help us."

"Help us how?"

"He called someone he knew with the local feds and they picked up Powers and his crew across the street from the hotel. They are all in custody now on the federal warrants."

Baker looked at her with astonishment. "Rick did that?"

"Well, his law enforcement contact did after he made a call."

"That's good then," Baker said, standing and pacing the room. "I do not know how Preston found us and so quickly, but that doesn't matter now. Finally, we are free of them and won't have to run anymore. I'm sure Greenwood is broke by now, so I doubt he'll give us anymore trouble. We're home free, Abby. Home free."

"Not quite," Abby said. "I found out more from Bishop."

Baker's smile disappeared, and his shoulders slumped again. He crossed the room and dropped back onto the edge of the bed. "What else did you learn?"

"The feds know we're in Honolulu and are looking for us, too. For all we know, they may have this place staked out now. And somehow, the feds have connected me with the heist, so they are looking for both of us now."

"Crap, Preston must have ratted you out to cut a deal," Baker said.

"Look, Alex, we haven't any time to waste. We have to get the money from wherever you hid it. Then we have to get off this island before the feds close in, or we could lose everything we've waited for the last five years."

"Okay, okay, let me think," Baker said, up and pacing again, running his hands through his hair. "Tomorrow is Sunday. We'll go get the money tomorrow morning when there won't be many people around downtown."

"No, Alex. Now. We have to go now. Don't you see? We can't wait until morning."

"Abby, we're talking about ten duffle bags stuffed with cash," Baker said. "I had to rent a van to move it when I arrived here. You seriously think we can make several trips in the rental car and carry the bags up here to the room tonight? That's crazy. We have to move the money once, from the hiding place to transportation out of Honolulu."

"But tomorrow morning might be too late."

That was a realistic fear for Abby, since Bishop told her he knew where the money was. She felt sure he had told her the truth, and she worried he might even now be loading up those duffle bags filled with cash that rightfully belonged to her. But she wouldn't share that tidbit of information with Alex because she still planned to rid herself of him and keep all the money. And he might do something stupid and get himself killed when she still didn't know where the money was. It had almost been within her grasp when that insane chick broke into Bishop's apartment. If they had sealed the deal, she and Bishop might have been loading those duffle bags of cash together right now.

"We have to wait until morning, Abby," Baker said firmly. "It isn't possible to get it tonight. First thing tomorrow morning, I'll hire a private jet to fly us out of Honolulu. Then we'll rent a van, get the money, and drive straight to the airport. We'll load the money into the plane and then take off immediately. It's the only way."

"We planned to take a ship. That's how you got the money here."

"No time for that," Baker said. "We'd be stuck with a ship's schedule and might stay moored at a dock for days with the cash onboard. If the feds are on our trail, they will check commercial flights and shipping. Hiring a private plane is the only way. And we can't do that tonight. Hell, we will be lucky to find someone to talk to about a plane in the morning since it's a Sunday."

Considering everything Alex had said, Abby reluctantly agreed. There were too many things they couldn't accomplish at night and, while risky, it seemed waiting until morning was the only option.

"All right, Alex. I know you're right. But I still don't like it. We're so close now and I keep thinking they might snatch our dream away just when we're almost free and clear."

"I know, sweetheart. I don't like waiting anymore than you do, but we have no choice."

"Okay," Abby said glumly, accepting it but still not liking it. "Then let's get some sleep and get an early start in the morning. While you arrange for a flight, I'll go out and rent a van. That way, when you've set it up, we'll be ready to roll."

Since nothing had happened with Bishop, she didn't need to shower, so Abby undressed and got into bed. Baker did the same and immediately joined her beneath the sheets and pressed himself against her. Then she felt his hand on her thigh and pushed it away.

"Not tonight, Alex. I can't even think of that again until we're on a plane tomorrow in the air with the money safely inside the cargo hold."

"Please, Abby," Baker begged.

She hated it when he did that. It made him appear so weak.

"I really need you tonight after what's happened, and I want us to reconnect."

"I said no, Alex. It's not happening tonight. Take care of it yourself if you must. But not in this bed. Go to the bathroom."

"Forget it," Alex said. "I'm sorry I asked."

Abby scooted away from him so he wasn't pressed against her butt. Baker rolled over with his back to her in a huff.

Men were all little boys with one-track minds, Abby thought. They always pouted when you told them no. Suddenly, she realized how disappointed she felt over what had happened with Bishop. Or what hadn't happened. She had so looked forward to a new conquest to escape the boredom of a steady diet of Alex Baker. And once she got his clothes off, Rick Bishop's merchandise had looked more than a little tantalizing. Yet all she got from it was frustration. Alex didn't know it yet, but they were finished. She and Alex would not be shaking the sheets together again, no matter how things turned out tomorrow. And she wasn't so sure she wouldn't make another run at Bishop if she got the chance.

CHAPTER TWENTY-EIGHT

Setting the Trap

ABBY WAS UP BEFORE seven on Sunday morning. After showering, she dressed in a loose-fitting pullover, black tights, and athletic shoes. She retrieved the handgun she'd taken from Preston in Maui and stuck it in the waistband of the tights at her back, covering it with the shirt. Then, after putting her hair into a ponytail, she donned a baseball cap. She waited impatiently until Alex emerged from the shower with a towel around his waist.

"I'm going to the airport to exchange the car for a van," she said. "Start calling at eight to see if you find us a plane."

"Okay," Baker said. "I'll call you if I get something set up before you get back."

"Do that," Abby said, and then she was out the door.

Before asking the valet to bring the rental out front, she walked the perimeter of the hotel but saw nothing suspicious. If the feds had set up surveillance, they were good because she didn't get a whiff of them. And with her training at the agency, she was good at spotting things that didn't feel or look right.

After the valet brought the car around, she got behind the wheel and left for the airport. She used every trick she had learned to uncover a tail, but again she spotted nothing suspicious, so she proceeded to Honolulu International. At the rental agency, she exchanged the car for a Hyundai minivan, and then left the airport for the hotel at 8:44. Her phone rang just as she merged onto the freeway. She answered after confirming it was Alex.

"I got us a Gulfstream G550 to Bangkok," Baker said. "Wheels up at eleven this morning. I told the guy we were transporting some property and looking to minimize import duties. He said he knows people at the airport there who will look the other way for a little scratch as long as I wasn't talking about narcotics. So, I think we're good to go with getting the money in there. The flight and the troubleshooting services at the Bangkok end are pricey, but under the circumstances we don't have time for bargain hunting."

"Yes, I agree," Abby said. "At this point, it would thrill me to get away with half the money and I just want off this island."

"Okay, you get the van?"

"Yes, I'm on the freeway now and on the way back. If the feds are surveilling us, they must be damn good, because I've seen nothing."

"Good, maybe Preston and his guys haven't told them much yet and we'll make it out of Honolulu without a problem."

"Be ready when I get there. I'll call you when I'm out front."

"Got it. See you then."

Abby ended the call.

Before falling asleep the night before, Abby had thought about how she would get rid of Baker once they picked up the money. Her preference was to do it in Honolulu after picking up the money and before boarding the plane. But with the tight schedule, she didn't feel confident she would have time to dump a body. It irritated her, but she would probably have to wait until Thailand. Still, it would likely be easier to take care of Alex there, anyway.

Bishop's phone woke him at 7:18 on Sunday morning. Groggily, he answered after his eyes focused enough for him to see the screen.

"Hey, bud, the woman is on the move in the rental," Utley said.

"You know where she is going?" Bishop said after clearing his throat.

"Airport it looks like," Utley said. "I've got four units on her and she has used every trick in the book trying to spot a tail. But my people are good. Last report, they said she seems sure no one is following her and looks like she's going to Honolulu International. I'm going to call TSA as soon as we hang up and tell them to detain her if she tries to board."

"She isn't getting on a flight," Bishop said. "Not without the money. My guess is she is on her way to swap the car for a van. Based on my calculations, they probably have eight to ten duffle bags to move. And that means they need a van."

"Huh, you might be right. So, you think no on the TSA?"

"Up to you, brother, you're the professional. But I'm certain she isn't going to the terminal. But your guys will let you know where she is going when they get there."

"True enough. So, what you have going today? Think we'll wrap this up?"

"Yes, if they are sourcing a van, they are going for the money. So, I'll call my HPD contact and rock and roll on my end of the plan. He wants it wrapped up by noon, so he'll be glad to get an early start. If your team verifies she has rented a van, hit me back when they tell you they are leaving the hotel in it."

"Will do. I'm in the field this morning, but you can get me at this number if you need to pass anything on from your end."

"Good to know. Talk to you later, bud."

Utley disconnected, and Bishop rolled out of bed. He took a quick shower and brushed his teeth. And then, while waiting for the coffee to brew, he called Chang.

"Good morning, Richard."

"Morning, David. Looks like Stone is on the way to the airport, probably to rent a van. So, we're ready to rock and roll. They will be on their way to get the money. As soon as we get to City Financial Tower, you can cut your patrol guys loose and call the fire department."

"All right, Richard. You leaving for there now?"

"In about five minutes."

"See you there."

"Yeah, see you, David."

Bishop pulled his filled commuter cup from the brewer tray and popped the lid on. Then he left the apartment. The Toyota's engine sputtered, coughed, and died four times before it finally caught and spluttered to life. The check engine light blinked on and off several times and then stayed on. Rick put the beast in gear and limped it out of the parking lot onto the street.

Fifteen minutes later, he parked on a side street, walked to the intersection, and then strolled down the sidewalk on Merchant Street. David Chang was standing at the entrance drinking coffee from a paper cup when Rick arrived at the City Financial Tower building.

"I sent the patrol guys home when I got here a few minutes ago," Chang said. "The back entrance is locked, and this is the only entry point."

Bishop nodded. "I haven't heard anything more from Utley since he woke me up this morning. So, they aren't on the way yet. But it shouldn't be much longer."

"Fire Department should be here any minute," Chang said.

Sure enough, two minutes later, a yellow HFD ladder truck turned on to Merchant Street and, with the hiss of air brakes, rolled to a stop in front of the building. A firefighter got out, walked around the truck, and lifted a hand to Bishop and Chang.

"Lieutenant Chang?"

"I'm Chang," David said.

"I'm Morris, apparatus officer. Where do you want us?"

Chang glanced at Bishop. "He's running the operation, so I'll let him tell you." Morris nodded.

"The truck is good where you are," Bishop said. "We want to simulate a response to a fire inside an office in this building."

"Any specific floor?"

"Sixteenth."

"Okay, no point in deploying the ladder. It doesn't go that high. We can run hoses inside the front entrance, which is what we'd actually have to do if the fire suppression system didn't handle it and we had to fight a fire up there."

"Sounds good," Bishop said. "But you needn't get carried away. A hose just inside the door will do what we need. I don't expect your guys to run hoses up to the office. And then if you have some barricades and fire line tape on your truck, that would be swell."

Morris nodded. "We can handle that. Mind if I ask what this is all about? The battalion chief said he didn't know other than we were helping HPD."

"We expect some bandits to show up here to pick up some stolen money from that office. We want to arrest them, but we don't want anyone getting shot if we can help it. So, we want to keep them out of the building. That's the purpose of the ruse."

"I see. Sounds fun."

"And if you don't mind, I'd like you to stand here with us when we hear they are coming. They will be mighty eager to get upstairs and I need you to explain about the fake fire and why that's too dangerous. You have knowledge I don't and it will sound more convincing coming from you."

"Okay, sure, no problem. But then how are you guys going to go about arresting them?"

"We won't," Chang said. "This is a federal case. The feds have them under surveillance and will follow them here. This is only a distraction to allow the feds to get their perimeter set up. They will take the suspects into custody."

"If you're convincing, we expect they will get back in their vehicle and try to drive away," Bishop said. "Then the federal agents will take it from there."

"Okay, we'll gear up and run out a hose. No reason to connect to a hydrant, I guess?"

"Well, you're the expert," Bishop said. "These people probably know less than I do about firefighting. But maybe a little water on the street would make things more convincing."

"Yeah, you're probably right," Morris said. "Okay, we'll connect to a hydrant and pump some water onto the street."

Morris turned and walked back to the truck, and gave his instructions. All the firefighters put on their gear. While two unrolled the hoses, another connected a hose to the pump intake and then hauled the other end towards a fire hydrant. Then two guys ran a hose inside the building through the front doors. Another firefighter strung the yellow plastic fire line tape while another set up folding barricades on the street behind and in front of the ladder truck. Then everyone stood around, waiting for the action to begin.

Bishop took his phone out of his pocket when it rang.

"The woman dropped off the passenger car and left the rental agency with a white Hyundai minivan," Utley said. "She's approaching the hotel now."

"Okay, we're ready and in position," Bishop said. "It shouldn't take them much over ten minutes to get here."

"You have the money?" Utley said.

"No, I'll wait until you get here and we'll all go up to the office together. But I'm sure it's there."

"What if you're wrong, bud, and the money isn't there and they don't head your way?"

"Then, by all means, improvise," Bishop said. "One way or the other, they will lead you to the money. I'm sure they are desperate to get to it this morning."

"Roger that," Utley said. "I'll let you know when I know."

Utley and Bishop rung off. Rick felt a little nervous. It would be embarrassing if he was wrong, and the money wasn't upstairs, hidden inside Alex Baker's fake private equity firm office. Maybe it would have been smarter to have gone upstairs to make sure. But when dealing with the federal government, it was always better to go straight by the book. Bishop knew Alex had spent some of the money. The only way Bishop could prove he had skimmed no cash off the top before turning it over was to go nowhere near the money until he had a federal representative along and it got counted. He wanted nothing getting between him and the reward he hoped to collect.

"Was that Agent Utley?" Chang said.

"Yeah, Abby Stone is almost back at the hotel with a van. Things will start popping soon."

"For your sake, Richard, I sure hope you're right about the money being upstairs. If not, we're all going to look pretty stupid."

"You got that right," Bishop said. "But I'm sure it's here. At least ninety-nine percent sure."

CHAPTER TWENTY-NINE

Rock and Roll

ALEX BAKER HADN'T WAITED for Stone's phone call. He was standing in front of the hotel entrance when she drove up in the van. Baker jumped into the front passenger seat.

"Let's do this," he said.

"Where am I driving us?"

"Downtown, to Merchant Street. There's a building called City Financial Tower where I leased an office for the private equity firm front."

"The money has been in the office all this time?" Abby asked with astonishment.

"It's been safe there, Abby. Come on. Get going. We have a plane to catch."

Abby nodded and drove out of the hotel driveway onto Uluniu Avenue and headed downtown.

"What is the plan when we get there?" Abby asked.

"I stashed two lightweight aluminum hand trucks with the money," Baker said. "We'll load five of the bags on each and then take them down the freight elevator to the back of the building. We only have to make one trip. Then we load the bags out the back into the van parked in the alley and head for the airport."

If Bishop hasn't already beat us to the punch, Abby thought pensively. The thought of it made her stomach roil. But she said nothing to Baker about that. She earnestly hoped that Bishop had lied about knowing where Alex had hidden the money, or at least that she and Baker arrived at the building before he did.

Bishop put his phone back into his pocket and looked at Chang.

"That was Utley," he said. "They are on the way. Stone and Baker left the hotel two minutes ago and are driving toward downtown."

"That's positive news, Richard," Chang said. "It seems your theory was correct."

"Yeah, it does," Bishop said with a sigh of relief. He had been highly confident he'd been right about the location of the money. But he reveled in getting confirmation finally.

Bishop walked over to Morris, who was standing with his guys at the ladder truck.

"Showtime," he said. "Do whatever it is you do when you've just finished extinguishing a fire."

Morris nodded and gave instructions to his crew of firefighters, then he followed Bishop back to the entrance of the building and they stood alongside Chang.

"What is my role in this play?" Chang said. "You've never said."

"You are Mr. Chang, the building rep who responded to the fire department's call about the awful fire," Bishop said with a grin. "But keep your weapon handy, in case they don't fall for the ruse. They both had weapons when I last saw them in Maui."

Chang nodded. And they waited.

Less than ten minutes later, a white Hyundai minivan turned onto Merchant Street from Bishop Street. The van driver signaled a right turn as if they intended to access the alley behind City Financial Tower. But then the van stopped abruptly in the traffic lane as if the fire truck, lights flashing, positioned in front of the building, had confused the driver. After the brief hesitation, the van continued up Merchant towards the building. Then the driver pulled to the curb short of the fire department's portable barricades and parked the van. Bishop and Chang watched intently to see what Stone and Baker would do.

"What do you make of this?" Abby said. "That fire truck is right out front of your office building."

"I don't know, Abby," Baker said nervously. "It looks like they are working a fire. I don't see any smoke, but there is a hose running into the building."

"Maybe they put it out already."

"We better walk over and find out what's what before we drive around back," Baker said, reaching for the door handle. "At least there are no cops around."

"Okay," Abby said, turning off the engine and getting out of the van. She suspected Bishop was behind this. But what had he done? Torched the place?

Baker and Stone walked past the barricades and up to a firefighter rolling up a fire hose.

"What happened?" Baker said.

Baker started when the man said, "Fire on the sixteenth floor."

"Bad?" Baker said.

The firefighter straightened up and looked at Baker.

"Are you the media?" he said.

"No, I'm a tenant. I have an office on the sixteenth floor."

"The guy standing over there is the apparatus officer," the firefighter said, pointing towards the building's entrance. "He can give you the details."

"Thanks," said Baker. Then he and Stone walked towards the entrance, avoiding the larger pools of water on the street.

"Damn it, that's Rick standing there," Baker muttered. "What the hell is he doing here?"

Stone felt sure she knew, but said nothing. She really had an upset stomach now.

"Here they come," Bishop said, watching Stone and Baker walking toward them. "I'd know those perfect hips anywhere. Let's rock and roll."

Stone and Baker stopped on the other side of the fire lane tape. Both wore casual clothes, complete with baseball caps and sunglasses. Because of the sunglasses, Bishop couldn't be sure Baker had glanced at him first before addressing Morris in his firefighter gear and helmet, but figured he had. And he could almost feel Abby's eyes behind her shades burning holes through him.

"What happened?" Baker said. "Was there a fire in the building?"

"Yes, there was," Morris said. "Sixteenth floor, but we've extinguished it. We're just setting up the exhaust fans now to remove the smoke and toxic fumes from the structure."

"I have an office on the sixteenth floor," Baker said excitedly. After reciting his office suite number, he continued. "Was it involved?"

"I'm afraid so," Morris said. "We've established the fire started there and damaged the offices on either side before we knocked it down."

"How bad?" Baker said.

"Worse than it should be," Morris said. "The fire suppression system failed, probably because of low water pressure. There must be a leak in the water line servicing the building."

"I'm David Chang, representing the owners of City Financial Tower," Chang said to Baker. "You're Mr. Baker?"

"That's right."

"Mr. Baker, were you storing flammable materials in your office suite?"

"Flammable materials? Of course not. There's nothing up there but office furnishings and my client files. Why?"

"Because," Morris said, "we found evidence of the use of an accelerant in your office suite. Gasoline probably. We're waiting for the arson investigator to arrive. But it looks cut and dried to me. We found localized burn patterns on the floors and surfaces and overhead damage inconsistent with the naturally available fuel. Someone purposely set the fire in your office suite. If we hadn't arrived when we did, we could have lost the entire building."

"I've got to get up there," Baker said, lifting the plastic tape and dipping beneath it. "I've got many confidential client files in the office."

Morris steeped in front of him, holding out his hands. "Sir, please move back behind the fire line. I explained your suite sustained heavy damage. The owners installed a drop ceiling during a renovation and the entire ceiling came down. Those materials are highly toxic when burned. My firefighters in there installing the exhaust fans are all wearing their self-contained breathing apparatus. There are also bare electrical wires after the insulation burned away."

"Before he left, the battalion commander told me even our insurance investigator can't enter the sixteenth floor until tomorrow at the earliest," Chang added helpfully. "It's too dangerous."

"But I must retrieve those files," Baker protested.

"Mr. Baker," Morris said sternly. "There are no files, no nothing. The fire incinerated everything. If you attempt to enter this scene, I'll get HPD out here and have you arrested."

Baker threw his hands into the air and then focused his frustration on Bishop.

"What the hell are you doing here, anyway?"

A hint of a smile appeared on Bishop's lips. "I came down here for the same reason you and Abby did. Sadly, it looks like we're all late to the party."

"You did this," Baker growled. "You burned my office to get even."

Bishop lifted his open hands in a WTF gesture. "I did no such thing, Alex. The fire department was already here battling the fire when I arrived just after five this morning. Frankly, I thought you probably torched the place to cover your tracks after retrieving what you came here to get. Actually, I think it's funny everything burned up. You're out of luck, pal."

Baker clenched his fists and glared at Bishop. Stone stood beside Baker with a hand covering her open mouth. Then on cue, sirens blared close by, Utley's signal to Bishop that the feds were in place for the take down.

Startled by the wailing sirens that had suddenly started, both Stone and Baker jumped involuntarily.

"I may have tipped off the feds when I saw you drive up," Bishop said flatly. "You two might want to make yourselves scarce. Sounds like they're pretty close."

Stone and Baker looked at each other for a moment in disbelief and then both turned and sprinted towards the van.

When they reached the van, they jumped in, with Abby behind the wheel. She whipped the van around in a turnabout with squealing tires and floored it towards Bishop Street. Then, as the van approached the intersection, it nosed down, and the tires screeched when Abby slammed on the brakes. Multiple sedans and sports utility vehicles with sirens wailing and flashing red and blue lights in the grills and on the dashes converged on the intersection from all directions. Federal agents wearing ballistic vests and raid jackets poured out of the vehicles like angry bees from a hive, all pointing firearms at the white van. Bob Utley's voice boomed over a public address system.

"Alex Baker and Abigail Stone, you are under arrest on federal warrants. Exit the vehicle with your hands up. Do it now."

Bishop held his breath until both front doors of the van opened. Abby and Alex stepped out with their hands in the air. Utley on the PA ordered them to step forward, and after five paces, stopped them. He ordered them to lie down on the pavement with their ankles crossed and arms out to their sides, palms up. They complied and then Bishop watched multiple agents holstering their sidearms and converging on them. In about thirty seconds, the agents had handcuffed them, hauled them to their feet, and escorted each of them towards separate vehicles. Abby turned her head and looked back over her shoulder towards Bishop. Then the agents hustled them both into the backseats of the law enforcement vehicles.

CHAPTER THIRTY

Closing the Loop

THE FIRE TRUCK HAD departed the scene with all their props and federal agents had transported Abigail Stone and Alex Baker to federal lockup when Bob Utley joined Bishop and David Chang in front of the City Financial Tower building. Utley beamed.

"I love it when a plan comes together," he said.

"Right, Hannibal," Bishop said. "Let's go up and recover the government's money."

"If it's really there," Utley corrected him.

"It must be," Chang said. "Otherwise, why would Stone and Baker have shown up here?"

"You can't argue with his logic," Bishop said. "Believe me. I've tried."

Then the three men entered the building and took the elevator up to the sixteenth floor. At the door to Alex Baker's former office, Bishop produced the key, unlocked the door, and pushed it opened. Chang and Utley followed him inside. They passed through the outer office and straight into the inner office Baker had used.

"Tell me again how you tumbled to the location of the money," Utley said.

"The first time we talked, I asked Alex how his new business was doing. He told me his profits were *literally* through the roof. It took me a while to decipher it, but one day, something struck me. When I was here before, I remembered this office had a false ceiling. And it made sense Alex must have concealed the money inside it."

"Sort of Freudian slip?" Chang said.

"Exactly, Bishop said, setting a solid visitor's chair in the center of the large wooden desk. After climbing atop the desk, Bishop stepped up on the chair. He lifted and shifted to the side, one of the pristine white ceiling tiles. Then, using his phone as a flashlight, he stuck his head and shoulders through the square opening and shined the light around."

Chang and Utley heard Bishop say, "Eureka," although it was muffled since he had his head and shoulders through the opening in the ceiling.

"Is it there?" Utley shouted.

Bishop squatted, lowering his head and shoulders back below the ceiling. Chang and Utley saw an enormous smile on his face.

"You better believe it," he said. "It's hard to tell because he laid the duffle bags out the length of the ceiling, but it looks like there are nine or ten of them."

Then Bishop's head and shoulders disappeared back through the opening. A moment later, he reappeared and handed down a black nylon duffle bag to Utley and Chang. Utley set the bag on the floor next to the desk and opened it. He stuck a hand inside and brought out several loose banded bundles of one-hundred-dollar notes. Tossing them on the desk, he dug back into the bag and then withdrew a shrink-wrapped brick of U.S. currency.

"You did it, bud," he said to Bishop. "You actually pulled it off."

"Good work, Richard," Chang said.

The men spent almost fifteen minutes removing the rest of the duffle bags, ten in all, from the ceiling. Bishop also found two lightweight aluminum hand trucks stored inside the false ceiling. After checking the other nine bags, they found each contained only unopened shrink-wrapped bricks of cash. It seemed Baker had only made withdrawals from the first bag. That suggested they had recovered most of the original ten million.

Utley called his agents still outside the building and told them to come to the office to carry the duffle bags down to their vehicles.

"Soon as we get back to the base, we'll count it," Utley said. "Then I'll contact the Treasury so they can pick it up."

"And to give them the name of the solid citizen who recovered it for them," Bishop said.

Utley laughed. "Don't worry, bud. I'll take care of you."

The two men shook hands and then Utley left with his team and the last load of cash-filled duffle bags.

"Am I to understand your motivation in all this was to collect a reward, Richard?" Chang said.

"Well, of course I mostly wanted to do my duty to my country," Bishop said. "But if my government wants to show a little appreciation by giving me a small reward, who am I to argue?"

Chang shook his head. "Just make sure the government reimburses the city for the police and fire resources we expended."

"No worries, David," Bishop said. "Get me an invoice and I'll hand carry to it to Utley."

Chang and Bishop took the elevator back down and exited the building, going their separate ways. Bishop got in the Toyota and his phone dinged with an incoming text. He took it out and read the text, sent by Gabby Inouye.

Booty call. My place and make it snappy. I've got a charter to fly in four hours.

A second text arrived by the time he'd read the first, also from Gabby.

And park your oil leaking POS at the curb not in my driveway.

Bishop grinned. Then he flipped to his contact list and clicked the call button next to Gabby's name. He had thought Koko had probably filled Gabby in on the situation by now. Maybe not.

"Why are you calling?" Gabby said petulantly. "You know the deal. Now get it in gear, buster. I'm waiting. The deal is, I call and you haul."

"Yeah, Gabby, about that."

CHAPTER THIRTY-ONE

Epilogue

BISHOP SAT AT A table on the deck behind the Likelike Club with a cold bottle of Longboard Island Lager across from his best bud, Joe Rose.

"It's harsh, Richard," Rose said in a sincere, apologetic tone. "I'm sorry. But Koko doesn't want you in the bar. Now that we're business partners, I can't just pull rank and overrule her. She wanted to ban you outright. But we worked out a comprise. You must confine yourself out here on the deck when you're at the club and I have to serve you myself."

"It's okay, Joe," Bishop said with a sigh. "You know what they say about a woman scorned."

"Listen, Richard, it's still raw right now. But I know Koko loves you and she has ended it with Kahiau. You can win her back, pal, if you make the effort."

Bishop drank some beer.

"I don't think so, Joe. Our relationship failed for a reason, and the trust is long gone."

"Richard, everyone makes a mistake sometimes. I know how you're feeling. I've had women cheat on me, too. But love means accepting someone with all their flaws. No one's perfect. You've made mistakes, too. Who are you to judge Koko? Besides, you can never punish her more than she in punishing herself. Koko knows she blew it."

Bishop shook his head.

"You don't understand, buddy. Yeah, I could never trust Koko again. But she could never trust me, either. I'm not saying with whom, but I cheated on Koko too even before I knew she had cheated on me. That says we don't belong together. I don't want her back and she shouldn't want me back. I only hope someday we might rebuild the broken friendship."

Rose rubbed his face with hands and then met Bishop's eyes. "That's too bad, Richard, and I can't say you've surprised me by admitting that. I never believed you appreciated what you had with Koko enough."

"I can't argue with that, Joe. You're probably right. I've never done well with relationships, which I why I resisted dating Koko in the first place. I never wanted to hurt her. And I deserve all the pain she has caused me. I just hope I've learned something this time and become a better person for it."

"It's really sad, Richard. I was sure you and Koko had what it took to last. And even though she's angry now, the things she says sometimes make me believe she wants you back once she's processed everything."

"I don't see it happening, buddy," Bishop said. "But as they say, never say never."

Bora Bora, French Polynesia, three months later.

Bishop lay on his back on the king-size bed inside the luxurious over the water bungalow suite with a towel wrapped around his waist. He had chosen the same resort as the first time he and Koko had vacationed here. She loved Bora Bora. After a full day of swimming and snorkeling in the warm, turquoise waters of the bay, Rick had showered first and the hot water had felt good as it washed the salt and sweat from his tanned skin. Now he listened to her humming in the shower and willed her to hurry. Sure, they would both have to shower again before leaving for dinner, but Bishop intended to have his way with her when she returned to the bedroom. After all, they hadn't made love since waking that morning before heading to the beach. She would pretend to resist, saying she'd only just showered, but he knew she only loved teasing him and would be as ready as he was.

Bishop turned his head and looked toward the bathroom when she turned off the water. Soon, he murmured under his breath contentedly and then closed his eyes, relaxed, and waited. The U.S. Treasury reward payment had hit his bank a month ago. It turned out to be only $1.5 million instead of the two million he had hoped for. But what the heck? Rick Bishop had joined the millionaire club.

He felt her body weight as she climbed onto the bed and lay on her back beside him. He cracked an eye lid open and saw she was wearing only panties and a towel she had wrapped around her wet hair. She was so beautiful and Bishop was so happy that they had talked things through and it had all worked out despite what she had done to him.

"God, it is so beautiful here," she said, sighing contentedly. "I love it here so much. Thanks for bringing me."

"The pleasure is all mine," Bishop said, turning to look at her. "Dating the rich has its privileges."

She smiled and batted her eyes at him, knowing he was looking at her bare, perky breasts. "What's for dinner?" she said.

"Whatever you desire, babe."

"What do you desire?"

"You," Bishop said, slipping a hand between her soft, firm thighs.

Pushing his hand away, she said, "No way. I just showered. But hold that thought for when we get back from dinner."

"But I want it now," Bishop said, cupping her breast.

She laughed while pushing his hand away, but less forcefully this time. "We mustn't. We would have to shower all over again."

"True, but we could shower together to save time, not to mention water. And I'll wash your back if you wash mine."

"Rick, you're incorrigible and also insatiable. Don't you ever get enough?"

"Not of you."

Putting her arms behind her head, she groaned in annoyance, but was smiling. Rick knew the exasperation act was all a fake.

"What do you think that slut Abby will get when she goes to trial?"

"Hm, I think the charge carries up to twenty years and a substantial fine," Rick said.

"It would serve her right to get the full twenty for seducing my man. She's lucky to be in jail where I can't get my hands around her neck. But she won't look so fine when she gets out of prison in her mid-fifties after twenty years of doing hard time."

Bishop laughed. Oh, my. Aren't you the vindictive little vixen?

"But you love me, yes?"

"Of course I do, babe."

"I'm glad. Love you back."

"So, does that mean we're doing it before dinner?"

"Hm," she said, pretending to give the idea serious thought. "I don't think we should. I'm starving."

"Me too. I'm starving for you."

She giggled and covered her face with her hands.

"And you're damn lucky I love you after the cruel way you treated me," Bishop said in a serious tone.

She turned her head and looked at him with her big, serious eyes. "Must we talk about that?"

"No," Bishop said, laughing. "Actually, I know I'm the lucky one."

"Aw, that's sweet," she said, and Gabby Inouye turned on her side and draped her arm over Rick's towel covered hips before kissing him. Then she grabbed the towel and snatched it away.

"Oh, my," she said covering her mouth with a hand in feigned embarrassment. "You're a big one, aren't you?"

"See what you do to me?"

"Does that mean you'll always be available for my booty calls, sailor?"

"Yes, but I enjoy them more now that I'm doing it voluntarily."

Gabby laughed. Then she pulled the towel off her wet hair before bending her knees and slipping the panties down her hips and silky legs.

"Don't forget," she said with a wide grin.

"Don't forget what?"

"You promised to wash my back when we shower again."

"You got it."

"Mm, then c'mere tiger. *Rawr.*"

About Author

LARRY DARTER is an American writer of fiction, primarily of the mystery & detective and police procedural genres. He is best known for the nine novels written about the fictional Los Angeles private detective Malone. Darter has also written four novels based on the fictional character T. J. O'Sullivan, a female New Zealand ex-pat, working as a private investigator in Honolulu, Hawaii, three police procedural novels featuring the fictional character LAPD homicide detective Howard Drew, and four novels in a comically toned private investigator series featuring Honolulu PI Rick Bishop.

The son of a police officer, Darter, joined the U. S. Navy at age 17. After receiving a bachelor of science degree from the University of Central Oklahoma, Darter was commissioned a second lieutenant in the U.S. Army Reserves assigned to the infantry branch. After leaving military service as a captain, Darter became a police officer, working at agencies in Oklahoma and Texas before retiring with after over twenty years of law enforcement service.

Also By Larry Darter

Rick Bishop Novels

The Girl on the Beach
Dead End
Trouble in Paradise
Follow the Money

Malone Novels

Come What May
Fair Is Foul and Foul Is Fair
Cold Comfort
Foregone Conclusion
Live Long Day
Foul Play
Black Deeds
Perchance to Dream
What's Done is Done

T. J. O'Sullivan Novels

Mare's Nest
Honolulu Blues
The Chinese Tiger Ying
Frisky Business

Howard Drew Novels

Omerta
The Pendulum
Darker Angels

www.ingramcontent.com/pod-product-compliance
Lightning Source LLC
Chambersburg PA
CBHW051842170626
46807CB00003B/1298